SHOUT OUT FOR THE
FITZGERALD-
TROUTS

Also by Esta Spalding

SHOUT OUT FOR THE FITZGERALD-TROUTS

ESTA SPALDING

ILLUSTRATED BY

LEE GATLIN

tundra

Tundra Books, an imprint of Penguin Random House Canada Young
Readers, a Penguin Random House Company

Library and Archives Canada Cataloguing in Publication

Spalding, Esta, author
Shout out for the Fitzgerald-Trouts / Esta Spalding ; illustrated
by Lee Gatlin.

Issued in print and electronic formats.
ISBN 978-0-7352-6451-9 (hardcover).—ISBN 978-0-7352-6452-6
(EPUB)

I. Gatlin, Lee, illustrator II. Title.
PS8587.P214S56 2019   jC813'.54   C2018-903334-7

Published simultaneously in the United States of America by Tundra
Books of Northern New York, an imprint of Penguin Random House
Canada Young Readers, a Penguin Random House Company

Library of Congress Control Number: 2018946083

Edited by Lynne Missen
The artwork in this book was created with traditional and digital media.
The text was set in Stempel Garamond.

Printed and bound in Canada

www.penguinrandomhouse.ca

1   2   3   4   5   23 22 21 20 19

Penguin
Random House
tundra | TUNDRA BOOKS

For Kristin

SHOUT OUT FOR THE FITZGERALD-TROUTS

PROLOGUE

We had had a swim and we had eaten ginker cake and we were sitting on the rocks beside the Fitzgerald-Trout siblings' favorite fishing stream when they began to tell me their story. Kim, the oldest, spoke first. "Kimo and I think what happened to us should be called 'The Family Calamity,'" she said.

"*Family* because it had happened to the five of us," Kimo chimed in. "And *calamity* because that's a word for when things go really wrong."

"Did things really go that wrong?" I asked.

The childrens' five sets of eyes in their five brown faces looked at me like my question was absurd.

"Um, yes," said Kim in a voice that exposed just how hard she and her siblings found it trying to make a grown-up understand anything important. "We're only telling you this because we want to make sure that what happened to us doesn't happen to any other family, ever."

"Write that part down," said Toby, the youngest boy, pointing to my notebook. He was holding his baby sister, Penny, in his lap and she seemed to be nodding in agreement.

I was about to put pen to paper when Pippa added, "You should put the word *monster* in the name too, because a monster was definitely part of the problem."

"Yeah. Plus, it sounds way cooler." Toby grinned at his sister.

"Okay," I said. "'The Family Monster Calamity.'" I wrote it in big letters at the top of the first page of my notebook. "Tell me how it started."

That's when they all began to talk at once. Kimo said something about their boat being taken and Kim said, "It was all the secrets." I couldn't make out what Toby or Pippa were saying, but it didn't matter because as soon as the baby spoke, they all stopped talking.

"What did Penny say?" I asked them.

The baby herself answered, saying, "Wimo."

"She's talking about the limousine," Toby explained. He looked more than a little sheepish.

Kim stared at me gravely. "Penny's right. The limo was the first secret between us."

Pippa wiped her glasses on her T-shirt and said matter-of-factly, "The limo, yes, the limo. That's where you should start our story."

CHAPTER

I

Toby was sitting in the grass with the baby, watching her play with a stick, when a car, bigger than any car he'd ever seen, pulled into the parking lot next to them. It was as long as two cars put end-to-end and as black and shiny as the mask worn by the villain in the movie he and his sisters and brother had seen at the drive-in a few nights before. Thinking of that villain, Toby instinctively reached for the baby and pulled her closer.

But the baby had her own ideas. "No," she said, wriggling away from him. "My do it." She hated when any of her brothers or sisters tried to take control of her, especially when she was doing something as important as stirring her drool into the grass with a stick. Toby let her go and turned his attention back to the car. A woman climbed out of the back. She wore bright green high heels and a matching green jumpsuit made of something that looked like snakeskin. Toby thought about how snakes shed their skin and it occurred to him that perhaps the woman had collected some snake skins and sewed them together. Then he thought that was silly; a woman with a car this fancy wouldn't sew her own snake skins together. She would hire someone else to do it.

"You must be Toby," the woman said. "And this must be Penny. And this . . ." the woman pointed to the jar that sat beside Toby in the sand, "must be the famous goldfish, Goldie."

"You know us," Toby said. He didn't make

it sound like a question because he didn't want to hurt the woman's feelings if she was some adult he was supposed to recognize. Like the other Fitzgerald-Trout children, Toby had very little interest in grown-ups and didn't always keep track of the ones he was supposed to know.

"I have never seen a more handsome goldfish in my life," the woman continued, then she smiled. It was a snake's smile, showing no teeth at all. "I'm Clarice," she said, holding out her hand. "Clarice McGuffin."

Toby wiped his hand on his T-shirt the way his sister had taught him, then shook the woman's hand. "Toby," he said. "But you know that."

"I'll tell you what I don't know," said Clarice. "I don't know if Goldie has ever been in a limousine."

"Not with me," said Toby. "But he might have before. He hasn't always been mine."

"How about we show him?" asked Clarice. "Just in case. Would he like to take a look?"

Toby was absolutely sure that Goldie would like to take a look, because Goldie always wanted to do what Toby wanted to do, and Toby wanted to take a look. After all, Toby was interested in cars because he and his brother and sisters lived in one. Sure, there had been a short time once when they'd lived in a cabin at the edge of the ocean, and just this past summer, they'd lived for a few months on a fishing boat *on* the ocean, but they didn't have that boat anymore. Their little green car was their home and gave them the freedom to go anywhere they wanted.

At night, they parked at a campsite beside Pea Tree Beach, where they slept under the stars and swam in the morning, cooking their oatmeal breakfast over a familiar campfire. Toby was very happy with this arrangement, but he knew that his sister Kim was not, that she wanted some place bigger and more permanent to live. She had a to-do list and at the top of it was written *Find a house.* She spent a lot of time dreaming up crazy ways of finding one and Toby—like his brother, Kimo, and his sister Pippa—would be very happy if Kim were finally able to tick that item off her list.

Now, looking at the limo, Toby thought what a terrific home it would make. If the little green car was a house, then this limo was a mansion. I really should take a look inside, Toby thought. Then he remembered the baby. "What about Penny?"

"She can look too," Clarice said. "I know for a fact that babies love limousines."

"Hey, Penny." Toby got to his feet. "Let's check it out."

"My do it," said Penny, but she held up her arms to say that she wanted Toby to carry her. With one hand, Toby swung her onto his hip. With the other, he grabbed Goldie's jar. A second later, he was peering into the open door of the enormous car. It had a comfy, plush seat at the very back, but it also had a long soft seat that ran from the rear of the car up to the front, ending just behind the glass that divided the passengers from the driver, who was wearing a little black hat and staring out the front windshield. He turned to look at Toby, and Toby's first thought when he saw the man's face was of the full moon in the night sky, and how if you looked at it just right you saw the man in the moon peering down at you with big, round, liquid eyes and an open, surprised mouth. The man in the moon smiled at Toby and the boy smiled back. Then he turned to study the rest of the car.

Facing the long seat was a small counter with a sink full of ice. Poking out of the ice were cold cans of Uncle Ozo's soda pop and little cans of baby formula. Next to the sink was a plate of cookies and a package of teething biscuits. Toby knew about these because Penny—who had two new teeth—loved them. Above the counter a television set was playing something, but Toby couldn't quite tell what it was because he was still outside the car, looking in through the open door.

"Go ahead," said Clarice. "You can climb inside if you want."

Most children are taught by their parents never, ever to get into a stranger's car. But the Fitzgerald-Trouts did not live with their parents and so they had never been taught this important lesson. The three older children—Kim, who was twelve, and Kimo, who was only a few months younger, and even nine-year-old Pippa—had learned this rule from movies and stories, but Toby (who was not yet seven) did not know it. Still, something in him hesitated. He glanced back toward the ocean where Kim, Kimo, and Pippa were swimming. He could see them far off in the distance, though they looked more like buoys than people, their heads bobbing on the surface of the water as they rode up and over the waves that rolled into shore.

But then he saw that the TV was playing an animated cartoon, so he leaned further into the car to see what the show was about. It seemed to tell the story of a rabbit which had lost its ears. Toby set Goldie's jar down on the floor of the limo and watched the TV, hoping to find out what had happened to the rabbit's ears. He noticed that there was a car seat for a baby. Just at that moment Penny, who was still in Toby's arms, began to cry, and Toby saw that she was pointing at the teething biscuits. "Can Penny have one of those?" Toby asked.

"I'll open a package," offered Clarice, sliding past them into the car. "You try that." She pointed to a button beside Toby. He pushed it and heard a whooshing sound as the roof of the car began to slide back, opening an enormous window. Toby could see the tops of the palm trees that arched over the parking lot and beyond them the deep blue of a sky that went on forever.

"Cool," Toby said. "Our car doesn't do that."

He watched as a flock of puk-puk geese flew over the car honking at each other, making him wish that he could stick his head out of the window and try to touch the feathers on their bellies.

"Go ahead," Clarice said, gesturing that it was okay for him to fully enter the limousine. But some part of Toby held back. He did not want to get all the way inside that car. There was a rustling of plastic. Clarice was opening a package of teething biscuits for the baby, who clapped her hands.

"Do you want to go for a ride?" Clarice asked.

Toby looked down at Penny. For most of his life, Toby had been the youngest Fitzgerald-Trout, the one who had always been babysat by the others. Now that he was older and had a little sister, he was enjoying being the babysitter for the first time. And something in him wondered whether a good babysitter would take the baby for a ride in the limousine. He wished his older siblings were there to answer this question. He looked at the spot where his brother and sisters were swimming and saw that they were on their way back to shore. "Maybe another time," the boy said, scooping up the goldfish jar and stepping away from the vehicle.

"Nice to meet you," the woman said.

Toby stood with Penny on his hip and Goldie's jar in his hand. The driver gave a wave as he backed the car out of its spot. Then he drove away. What a car! thought Toby. I wish we had one. Kim could finally cross out those words on her to-do list.

Later that week, on Friday, Kim was sitting in her seventh grade classroom staring at this very to-do list. She was supposed to be listening to her teacher, Mr. Petty, who was standing at the chalkboard talking about island history, but instead Kim was studying the words *Find a house*.

"Kim? Kim? Are you pay-ing attention?"

"Yes," she answered,

before she even realized Mr. Petty was glaring at her.

"If you're paying attention, Kim, then stand up and tell me what I just said," Mr. Petty challenged.

"Ummm," Kim said. She thought that they had been talking about the explorer Captain Baker, but she wasn't entirely sure. As she rose to her feet, a cloud of birds flew through the classroom. (Because the Fitzgerald-Trouts lived on a tropical island, most of the classrooms at their school had no walls.) A few of the birds dropped mushimush berries on the floor, causing an eruption of giggles from the students. The birds and the laughter did nothing to distract Mr. Petty. He just shook his head and frowned.

He was a no-nonsense teacher who, despite the warm tropical weather, managed to have crisply pressed shirts and pants at all times. The kind of teacher who ironed his socks and always had a starched handkerchief in his pocket. On the first day of school, he'd told the class that he believed seventh grade should be very difficult. "I like to give pop quizzes and to make sure every student is comfortable with public speaking," he'd said. "I also assign mountains of homework every night. So prepare yourself." Kim, who always got straight As, wanted nothing more than to please her new teacher, but so far—four months into the school year—she had not succeeded. Because when you lived in a small car and were responsible for your four brothers and sisters, it was not easy to do mountains of homework every night or to practice public speaking or to study for pop quizzes.

Kim felt the eyes of the entire class focus on her. "Ummm," she said again. She wanted to say the name "Captain Baker," but the words weren't coming out.

"What? Speak clearly, Kim. Enunciate."

Kim's throat was dry. She felt the eyes of her classmates on her. She looked at the chalkboard, hoping that if she didn't look at her classmates, the words might emerge. Seated at the desk next to Kim's, Violet Cringle raised her delicate hand. "Can I help, Mr. Petty?"

"Yes, Violet, thank you."

Kim sat back down as Violet chirped, "We were talking about exploration. We were talking about the first Europeans who arrived on the island two hundred years ago."

Captain Baker, Kim said again in her head. Kim had stayed up later than her brothers and sisters, reading with her textbook on island history propped on the steering wheel and a flashlight between her teeth.

"That's right, Violet," Mr. Petty was saying. "We were talking about Captain Baker, who arrived on the island in his ship, the *Billy Goat*. He loved the island so much he decided to stay here. In 1785, Captain Baker built a house on the slopes of Mount Muldoon. Turn to page one-forty-six in your textbook."

And that's when a wonderful thing happened, a thing that the Fitzgerald-Trout children later told me completely changed their lives: Mr. Petty asked the class to read the description of the house that Captain Baker had built.

Kim flipped open her worn textbook. On page 146, there was a large brown crust of chocolate left by a former seventh grader. Beneath it, Kim could just barely make out the following words: "Captain Baker wanted his house to be as tall as the tallest ship he had ever sailed, so he made it three stories high and built it out of volcanic stone. There were thirty-three rooms (all of them had large fireplaces) and that included a living room, a dining room, an observatory, and a kitchen." As the class read aloud, Kim began to picture the Captain's magnificent house.

He built a library with bookshelves from floor to ceiling and an enormous bay window that looked out over the island. From that window, the Captain could watch the fishing canoes sail in and out of the Bay of Hanalee; across the ravine he

could see the waterfall at Makapepe; and he could
observe the taro farmers, knee-deep in mud, plant-
ing and picking their crops that grew in the marshes
on the edge of the Sakahatchi.

Kim pictured the view as Captain Baker would have seen it. The island was busier now, but the bay was still there, as well as the waterfall and the marshes. In fact, the view seemed almost familiar to Kim. If she hadn't stood exactly in that spot on Mount Muldoon, she had certainly been near it. She'd swum in the pool beneath the Makapepe waterfall many times and picked guavas from the trees that grew around it. Kim definitely thought she knew which trail up the mountain led close to the place where you could see Hanalee on your right, the waterfall across the ravine, and the marshes of the Sakahatchi stretched out at your feet.

If that was true, it meant Kim knew the trail that led close to the place where the house had been. Or still was. Because wouldn't a house built from volcanic stone still be standing even if the house had been built more than two hundred years ago?

Kim thought about asking Mr. Petty this question, but then she thought better of it. She didn't want to try to speak out loud in front of the class again, and besides, she had learned that if you could avoid consulting a grown-up about something, then you definitely should. Grown-ups had a way of making everything difficult. Take their parents, for example. Between them, the Fitzgerald-Trout children had five different mothers and fathers. Their family tree was impossible to keep track of, but the one thing that was clear was that all five of their parents were terrible. For instance, none of them had ever given the children a place to call home; instead, those five parents had left the children to fend for themselves and live on their own in the little green car that they parked at the beach.

Of course it was true that the children's parents were so terrible that the Fitzgerald-Trouts considered themselves lucky not to have to live with any of them. Kim, Pippa, and Toby would not have wanted to live with their father, Dr. Fitzgerald, a scientist who many years before had moved them all into the car before flying off to a different, distant island to pursue his research. Nor would they have wanted to live with greedy Maya, Pippa and Kim's mother, who had been found guilty of stealing billions of dollars. Living with Maya would have meant living in a very small jail cell.

Kimo, Toby, and Penny's mother was Tina, a country-and-western singer whose songs sometimes topped the island's music charts. She was so famous on the island that she had begun to travel with a team of bodyguards. She had no time for the children, and her only attempt at parenting was to leave them a monthly envelope of money in the glove compartment of the car. She cared for them so little that the year before she had left her most

recent offspring, the baby, Penny, in the backseat of the car.

Penny's father was Tina's husband, a man named Clive who wore a blue tuxedo and drove a matching blue convertible. He was not only bored by the baby, he was scared of her; somehow he'd even convinced himself he was allergic to Penny because the one time he'd held her he'd broken out in hives.

These four parents were certainly terrible, but the fifth parent—Kimo's father, Johnny Trout—was the most terrible of all. Not only had he never offered the children a place to live, he had actually stolen the boat that they'd won in a contest. It had happened a few months before. The Fitzgerald-Trouts had been at the laundromat doing their laundry and watching their favorite TV game show, *Ham!* The vending machine at the laundromat had been broken, so they'd had free chocolate bars to stuff into their mouths while they watched the contestants on *Ham!* stuff sausages into *their* mouths and tell jokes. Kim and her siblings had had a very good time and they were all laughing and repeating the jokes as they left the laundromat and drove down the road to the wharf where their fishing boat was docked. Kim had turned the car into the parking lot and that's when they had seen it: the boat, up in the air, hanging by a few thin wires from the end of a crane.

Kimo was the first out of the car, running across the gravel lot and shouting at the man seated in the crane, operating the levers. "What are you doing?" The man stopped moving the levers and got up from his seat. He came over to Kimo and handed him a piece of paper. It was a letter from a judge saying that Kimo's father, Johnny Trout, had sued and that the judge was ordering that the boat be locked up until ownership was properly determined by the island's courts.

"When's that gonna be?"

The man shrugged. "We locked one up last year and it's still there. The courts are slow."

The children looked at each other. A year? It was too awful to believe. But there was nothing they could do, so they just stood staring up at the boat's wet hull as water dripped off it like tears, and Kim vowed to her siblings that they would find another place to live.

But she hadn't had any luck—until now. Was she right to think that Captain Baker's house, a house built from volcanic stone, would still be standing after two hundred years? We'll find out, she thought. We'll hike that trail, and maybe we really will do the most important thing on my to-do list! Kim's reverie was interrupted by the sound of the bell ringing.

"Be sure to read chapters five and six," Mr. Petty announced as the students began to gather their books and head for the door. "There'll be an oral test on Monday. You'll stand and recite your answers for me."

On Monday I'll have to stand in front of the class and recite answers, Kim thought with terror. Then she cheered herself up, thinking: maybe by Monday we'll have a house.

The bell had rung, but Pippa didn't care. She was in her woodworking class, where her teacher, Mr. Bragg, let her stay after school to work on projects.

She waved goodbye to the other kids and grabbed a plastic visor, then she carried the pieces of wood that she had measured over to the table saw. Mr. Bragg, who spent his weekends cow wrangling and insisted on being called Bronco Bragg, helped her turn on the saw. He watched as Pippa, paying careful attention to the line she'd drawn, pushed the wood slowly against the spinning blade. When Bronco Bragg saw that she was using the machine properly, he patted her on the head (like she was one of his ponies) and said, "Giddyap."

Just then Pippa spotted Kim heading into the room. The look on Kim's face told Pippa that her older sister was in a hurry. But before Kim could say anything, Pippa bent over the wood and began to make the next cut. She loved the feeling of the blade making contact with the wood, the teeth biting in and cutting, the sawdust flying. She was very careful to keep her fingers away from the saw—just as Bronco Bragg had taught her—but she knew that Kim was holding her breath, worried her little sister would cut her fingers. Kim's worrying drove Pippa crazy, since Pippa was perfectly capable of taking care of herself. When the wood was cut, she flipped off the saw. "It's time to go," Kim said before the noise had even died down.

"I've got another piece to cut," Pippa replied, wiping the wood dust from her safety goggles.

"I've got a plan," Kim said.

But instead of exciting Pippa, this pronouncement only made her groan. "Another plan?"

"Don't be negative," Kim said. "This plan is gonna work."

"I'm not negative," said Pippa. "I'm busy. I'm making a knickknack shelf."

"What's a knickknack shelf?" asked Kim.

"It's a shelf where you put things that you collect."

"What do you collect?" Kim was annoyed now.

"Nothing yet," said Pippa. "But when I have a shelf, I will."

"And where will you hang the shelf?" Kim prodded because she knew the answer.

"I don't care if I don't have anywhere to hang it," said Pippa. "I'm making it anyway."

Kim read the fierce expression on her little sister's freckled face and her heart went out to her. "I want you to have a place to hang it," Kim said. Pippa narrowed her eyes, and Kim grinned. "Finish what you're doing. I'll go find Kimo."

A few minutes later, Kim found Kimo on the athletic field, running down the track holding a long flexible pole. He had taken up pole vaulting a month before, and in that short time it had become his consuming passion. Kimo was a speedy runner with enormous upper body strength, and the combination was perfect for a pole vaulter. In fact, the first time he'd tried the sport—during a PE class—he had used the rubber pole for beginners but had cleared the nine-foot mark. He'd tried again with the real pole and gone up and over the twelve-foot mark. Ms. Bonicle, his PE teacher, shook her head and said that couldn't be right. "Try again," she said.

This time Kimo flew fourteen feet and two inches into the air. So the number hadn't been wrong. And that was when Ms. Bonicle said, "The island record for pole vaulting is fifteen feet, two inches. You keep practicing, and you're gonna break that record." Kimo had kept practicing and he was now within five inches of the island record.

Kim watched as Kimo finished his sprint by planting the tip of the flexible pole in a pit and using the pole's bend to flip himself up and over the bar. He came sailing down through the air and flopped onto the deep, soft mat. Kim raced over. She was out of breath before she even reached him. "How high?"

"Fourteen feet, eleven inches," Kimo said matter-of-factly.

"Wow!" Kim was genuinely impressed with her brother. Though they had different mothers and different fathers and though Kimo wasn't yet in seventh grade, the two of them had always thought of themselves as being like twins. After all, weren't they nearly the same age? And weren't their names almost identical—only one letter different? And didn't one often seem to know exactly what the other was thinking? But now, when Kim watched Kimo fly through the air, she saw how entirely different the two of them were. "You really might break that record," Kim said.

Kimo only shrugged. "I've got work to do before that happens." What Kimo didn't say to Kim was that he was willing to do every bit of the hard work that it would take because he was sure that if he broke the island record, there would be an article about him in the newspaper, and that meant his father would see the article and read about Kimo's great achievement. Even though Kimo's father, Johnny Trout, had never paid any attention to his son, Kimo thought his father might pay attention to an island record. His father might even be proud of his son for breaking that record. And maybe, just maybe, that meant that Johnny Trout would consider dropping his lawsuit and giving Kimo and his siblings back the fishing boat. Kimo picked up the pole and started back toward the beginning of the track to try again.

"Wait," Kim said. "You have to stop." Kimo looked at her, puzzled. "Something big has happened," she continued. "Something important." Kimo furrowed his brow. What could be more important than breaking the island pole vaulting record?

"Pippa's gonna be here any minute. We have to find Toby, and pick Penny up from day care."

Kim was breathless again—this time with excitement. "I think I might know how to find a house."

Kimo gave her a huge grin. "Yeah?"

"Yes," she said, gratified that he looked pleased. Then she added, "We need to get going now—while it's still light out."

"Where are we going?" Kimo asked, then before Kim could answer, he added, "Not the Sakahatchi, I hope." He was remembering the drive Kim made them take through the forest of bloodsucking iguanas one time when they'd been looking for a house.

"Not the Sakahatchi," Kim said. "Above the Sakahatchi, on Mount Muldoon."

"Wait," said Kimo, shuddering and shaking his head. "The trails on that side? Don't they go super close to Gasper's Gulch?" They both knew what Kimo meant. Gasper's Gulch was a breeding ground for wizzleroaches, and Kimo hated the six-legged, flying insects more than anything. "If I see a single wizzleroach, I'm blaming you," Kimo said darkly.

"Fine." Kim didn't argue. Kimo could blame her all he wanted once they got to Captain Baker's house.

CHAPTER

2

W hat's the deal with you and wizzleroaches anyway?" Pippa had her feet up on Kimo's seat and was pressing into his back.

"Dunno," he said, pushing against her and adding, "Cut it out!" He stared out the window at the long, straight stretch of road that ran from their school to the base of Mount Muldoon, where they planned to park the car and begin their hike into the forest that might or might not take them close to wizzleroaches. "I think it's the sound of their feet," he mused. "It makes me feel itchy, like my skin has creepy crawlers all over it."

Baby Penny in her car seat must have recognized the word "feet" because she grabbed her own in both her hands and proudly shouted, "Fee!"

"The best animals don't have any feet at all," Toby offered, peering into the jar that held Goldie and admiring the goldfish's elegant orange fins. Then he thought very hard, *Fish are the best pets.* He was training Goldie to read his thoughts and so far it seemed to be working; Goldie stared out of the jar in a way that made Toby sure he had understood.

Kim got a glimpse of this in the rearview mirror and it made her grip the steering wheel and fight the instinct to snap at Toby. She had to work to be nice to her littlest brother, who could drive her crazy. "Please," she said, "let's talk about Captain Baker's house. The book says it has thirty-three rooms and that every room has a fireplace."

"*Had*," Pippa said, her dark freckles flaring.

Those freckles had a way of underlining Pippa's temper, which was always threatening to explode. "The house *had* thirty-three rooms that each *had* a fireplace, two hundred years ago when Captain Baker built it. We aren't gonna find that house," said Pippa. "If we do, I'll be a monkey's uncle."

"I'd like to see that," said Toby. "*Oo-ooh, aa-aah.*" He scratched his armpits and mimicked being a monkey. "If we find it, you have to do that, what I just did, till we tell you to stop."

"Sure," said Pippa. "Whatever." And that's when Kim realized what was going on. Her brothers and sister were talking about monkeys' uncles and wizzleroaches because too many times in the past they had lost the homes they cared about: the cabin on the cliff, the fishing boat. They were willing to look for another place now, but they didn't want to get their hopes up about it, and they absolutely would not allow themselves to imagine living in Captain Baker's house until they were actually standing inside its walls of volcanic stone, staring out the bay window with Hanalee on the right, the waterfall across the ravine, and the marshes of the Sakahatchi stretched in front of them.

"Thanks for going along with this," Kim said, suddenly full of love for her siblings.

"Of course," said Kimo. "We're Fitzgerald-Trouts. We don't give up and we don't back down."

"Unless there's a wizzleroach," Pippa quipped. This made all of them laugh, including the baby, whose laughter always turned into a long spiral of drool.

Pippa grabbed an old T-shirt to mop the baby up as Kimo asked, "Where's that history book?" Toby got the textbook from Kim's backpack and handed it to Kimo, who flipped it open to the chocolate-covered page. He read for a minute, then looked up. "Do we still have the compass?"

"It's in the trunk," said Kim, "with all the stuff the harbormaster took off the boat before the judge confiscated it."

"Good," said Kimo. "We'll follow the trail to the waterfall, then use the compass from there."

"It's like a treasure hunt," Toby enthused. "Only there might be a house at the end of it."

Just then baby Penny began to wail—the sound that meant she wanted her bottle, which was in the cooler in the trunk.

"We can't pull over here," Kim observed. "The road's too narrow."

"Put on the radio," Pippa suggested. "That always distracts her." But when Kimo snapped on the radio the first voice they heard was a voice that didn't distract any of them; it was the voice of their mother, Tina, the country-and-western singer. "Another terrible tune by terrible Tina," Pippa groaned, adjusting her glasses on her nose.

"It's not a tune," said Kim, who had heard it in the grocery store a few days before. "It's an advertisement."

They all leaned a little closer to the radio as Tina crooned, "Baby loves veggies, baby loves meat. Baby loves fruit, and good things to eat. Baby loves Mommy and baby loves Dad, when baby sees that Baby Loves is what she's gonna have . . ." It was a jingle for a line of baby food from a company called Baby Loves. The children knew all about Baby Loves because since Penny had been left in their care, they had bought a lot of Baby Loves baby food, and they had also bought a lot of Baby Loves diapers and Baby Loves baby shampoo and baby powder and, most recently, Baby Loves teething biscuits because Penny had her third tooth coming in.

The irony that Tina—who had left her baby with her other abandoned children—was singing a jingle for a product called Baby Loves was not lost on the Fitzgerald-Trouts. "Remember the bag

of diapers Tina left in the car with Penny? Those were Baby Loves diapers," Kimo snarled.

"She probably got them for free," said Pippa.

"I bet she's friends with that lady who owns Baby Loves," Kim offered. She knew the face of Clarice McGuffin, the president and owner of Baby Loves, because it was plastered all over the island on billboards that showed her tight-lipped smile as she held up a box of Baby Loves diapers or a jar of Baby Loves baby food or a package of Baby Loves teething biscuits. "That lady gives me the creeps," said Kim. "Why does she have a picture of herself on her billboards and not a picture of a baby?"

"Those billboards are the worst," said Pippa. "She uses Comic Sans." Pippa was an expert on computer fonts and absolutely hated signs or documents that were printed in Comic Sans, which she considered tacky. "If that isn't bad enough, she wears a jumpsuit made from snakeskin."

Toby, who had only been half-listening, suddenly turned to Pippa. "She wears what?"

"A green snakeskin suit. Why?"

"No reason," said Toby, who had only just realized that the woman from the billboards was the same woman whose limousine he'd looked at a few days before. No wonder there was baby formula in the sink, Toby thought. No wonder there were teething biscuits. For fear of losing his babysitting privileges, Toby had not mentioned the limousine to his sisters and brother. So now, instead of admitting that he'd met Clarice, he lamely offered, "Snakes don't have feet."

"Oh, Clarice has feet," said Pippa. "She wears snakeskin high heels."

Kim looked down at her feet which, like all the other children's on the island, were bare. "Why would anyone wear those?"

"She wears them because she likes to be scary," said Pippa.

Before he could stop himself, Toby said, "She's not scary." Then he waited nervously to see if any of his siblings would ask him how he knew. But they didn't. They thought Toby was only talking about Clarice's appearance on the billboards.

"She is too scary," Pippa said. "Her smile on those billboards is downright creepy."

"She must be nice, though. She loves babies," said Kimo.

"She *says* she loves babies, but we just heard Tina sing about loving babies, and if there's anybody who doesn't love babies, it's Tina." Pippa let out a sinister laugh.

The road was beginning its climb up the mountain, so Kim pressed harder on the gas. The engine made a terrible grinding noise and then a sound like a cough. And then another cough. "It sounds sick," Kim whispered to Kimo. "It needs a mechanic." They knew they didn't have enough money to repair the car.

"Maybe it needs a doctor." Kimo tried a joke, but Kim didn't laugh.

Almost as if she felt her sister's worry, Penny began to cry again. Pippa turned in her seat and tried to distract her little sister with her favorite toy, a dirty, bedraggled, stuffed octopus.

"Look at your octopus. Isn't he happy, huh? Happy!" The octopus did not look happy at all; in fact, one plastic eye hung by a few threads from the animal's face, and the other was completely gone. Penny wailed again, as if voicing the octo-pus's pain.

"Baby Loves getting out of the car," Kim said as she swung the car into the parking lot marked Muldoon Park Parking Lot.

"Weird," said Pippa. "A park is a place full of grass and trees and it's also the thing you do to stop your car. But they have nothing to do with each other. Can someone explain to me why they're the same word?" She shrugged and shook her head. "Another ridiculous rule made by a grown-up."

A few minutes later, the Fitzgerald-Trouts climbed out of the car at the far end of the parking lot, near the spot where two trails up the mountain began. While Pippa sat Penny down on the grass and gave her a bottle, Kim and Kimo passed a bag of potato chips back and forth and studied the map of the park that was posted on a tall wooden sign.

"We should take the left trail . . ." Kimo ran his finger along it. "That way, we'll end up on the southern side of Muldoon, where you can see the bay and the Sakahatchi."

"If you take the right trail," Kim argued, "you can still see the bay, but you end up closer to the waterfall." As Toby watched his older siblings, it occurred to him that Kimo had chosen the trail that ran farther from Gasper's Gulch. He lifted the goldfish's jar and thought very hard, *Kimo doesn't want to go near the wizzleroaches.* He could see that Goldie was thinking the same thing.

"You can see the waterfall from here." Kim licked the broken pieces of potato chip off her finger and tapped on a spot on the map.

"Maybe," said Kimo. "But definitely from here." He pointed to a different spot, and Toby saw that Kimo's spot was most certainly farther from the gulch.

Pippa came over with the baby, who was now smiling and sucking on one arm of her octopus. "We can't take your route, Kimo." Pippa was already studying the map.

"Why not?"

"See how it goes past that old safari place?" Pippa grabbed the bag of chips while the others leaned in closer to look at the *X* on the map that marked the Wildlife Safari Park. It was a zoo that offered jeep rides through a large, fenced-in area filled with giraffes, zebras, and elephants. "Lehua Madigan told me that her family tried to go a few weeks ago, but the place was closed down. She said they wandered around but there was nothing there. No jeeps, no animals, nothing. Remember how they used to have that candy store—The Fudge Factory? Even that was gone. Lehua said the whole place got wrecked in one of the floods last summer and now it's like a ghost town."

"Ghost town?" Toby lowered his voice. It wasn't clear if he was spooked or excited.

"Ghost town doesn't mean there's really ghosts," said Kim. "It just means the place is super empty."

"So what if it's empty?" asked Kimo.

"It's not that it's empty," said Pippa. "It's that if the park was flooded, then the trail you want to take was flooded too. It's probably washed away completely."

"Or at least so badly marked we won't be able to follow it." Kim saw Pippa's logic. The two sisters smiled at each other. It was a rare moment when they were in agreement.

"Sorry, Kimo." Toby poked his older brother in the shoulder. "We've gotta go close to the wizzleroaches." The others burst out laughing when they realized what Toby had known all along: Kimo wanted to avoid the gulch.

Pippa turned to Kimo. "Roasted by Toby."

"No kidding," said Kimo.

Toby smiled and snatched the bag of chips. "Gimme those."

"Everybody ready?" Kim adjusted the backpack that she had loaded with extra gear—food, bottles of water and baby formula, toothbrushes, a

Swiss Army knife, a flashlight, the textbook—and pulled out the compass.

"Wait," said Pippa, looking up at the sky and realizing the sun was already on the other side of Mount Muldoon. "It's too late to leave. It's four o'clock. The sun sets at six. What happens if we don't find the place before dark? We won't be able to hike back down."

"It's not that far," said Kim, who was resolved to get going. "It won't take us two hours."

Kimo nodded. "I think we should go."

"Goldie's saying yes," said Toby, who was staring at the fish and trying to read its mind.

"My do it," shouted Penny, sensing the spirit of the moment.

"Okay," said Pippa, grimacing in a way that made her freckles darken. "I hope you guys are right." She held out Penny to Kimo, who took the baby and slung her up onto his shoulders.

"This'll give me a good workout," he said as he started toward the trail. He began to chant, "Give a loud shout 'cause we're Fitzgerald-Trouts. We . . ." He trailed off. He couldn't think of a next line.

But remembering Kimo's words in the car, Kim chimed in, "Don't give up. We don't give in. We . . ."

"Eat chips," interrupted Toby, who had turned the potato chip bag inside out and was licking it to get the last of the salt.

"And sauerkraut," said Kimo.

"And gin," Pippa shouted out.

"Gin? We've never had gin in our lives," retorted Kim.

"We've never had sauerkraut either," said Pippa. "But *gin* rhymes with *in*."

Kimo put the whole chant together. "Give a loud shout 'cause we're Fitzgerald-Trouts. We don't give up and we don't give in. We eat chips and sauerkraut and gin. And now we start the chant all over again . . . Give a loud shout 'cause we're Fitzgerald-Trouts . . ." Soon they were all repeating the words over and over, their voices carrying across the forest as they followed the steep trail up the mountain.

By the time they had reached the last switchback to the top of Gasper's Gulch, they were all wondering if Pippa had been right when she'd said that it was too late to leave. The sun lay far below the mountain and the purple evening was pouring into the gaps of sky between the tree branches. There was no chanting now. They walked in silence, except for Penny, who had begun to whine and wouldn't be soothed even by a Baby Loves teething biscuit. Kim caught up to Kimo—who was still carrying the baby—and walked beside him for a minute.

"What do you think?" she asked.

He shook his head in a worried way, and Kim followed the thread of Kimo's thinking and realized that he probably wasn't concerned about the time, he was probably concerned about the possibility of wizzleroaches. "I'll go first," she said. "I'll let you know if I see any." She strode out ahead and crested the hill, looking down toward the gulch with a gasp. "Whoa," she said. "Slow down."

They all came to a stop and looked where she was looking. The gulch wasn't there anymore; where it had once been was a space now filled with dark black rock.

"Lava," said Pippa. "From this summer." They knew what she meant. Over the summer there had been a series of volcanic eruptions from Mount Muldoon. Lava from the eruptions had poured down the volcano and where it had flowed it filled in mountain's crevices, including Gasper's Gulch. Now that lava was hardened to stone.

"Which way is the trail?" Kimo asked.

"No way," Kim said. "It's covered with hard lava."

They stood in silence. None of them had any idea which direction they should go in. At last Pippa said, "Let's split up in pairs and look for where the trail picks up again."

"Good idea," said Kimo. "Shout if you find something. Otherwise, we'll meet back here in, say, about ten minutes."

"How long is ten minutes?" asked Toby.

"The time it takes for water to boil in a pan on the campfire," offered Kimo. They all knew exactly how long that was. So without another word, they took off in different directions. Kimo and Pippa headed uphill following the seam of black rock, hoping that the trail would reappear. Kimo was holding Penny and singing silly rhymes to entertain her. "Give a loud shout 'cause we're Fitzgerald-Trouts. We don't give up and we don't give in. We eat ketchup with sauce and play violin."

Kim and Toby climbed right up onto the black rock itself. Kim thought if they crossed the rock in the right direction, they might find the continuation of the trail on the other side. But the rock covered such a wide area that by the time they got to the other side, there was no sign of the trail at all. Ten minutes later, she and Toby were back at the original spot, only now the sky was that much darker; the night, that much closer.

"Go ahead and say it," said Kim as Pippa appeared with Kimo and the baby. "Say, 'I told you so.'"

But Pippa just shrugged. "I'm not glad to be right." Then she added, "We should hike back down to the car while there's still a little light."

But Toby didn't think so. He was holding up Goldie's jar and peering in at the goldfish. "Goldie thinks we should find a place to camp for the night," the boy said.

"Not a bad idea," said Kimo. "Tomorrow's Saturday. We can keep looking for as long as we want."

"So we're taking suggestions from a goldfish now?" Pippa snarked, but she didn't disagree.

"We need to find a sheltered place to camp," offered Kim, but the last word became a shriek of surprise as a pair of black wings swooped out

of the darkness and flew past her ear. "What was that?"

"A bat," declared Kimo. Then as another pair of wings and another and another filled the air around them, he amended his observation. "Bats. Lots of 'em!"

"They're coming from up there." This was Pippa, pointing up the hill to a break in the trees. The bats were coming through it and scattering like black ink spilled across the bruised sky.

"Get me outta here." Toby turned to run.

"No," said Pippa. "That's exactly where we need to go." The others looked at her like she'd lost her wits. "Don't you get it?" Pippa said. "Where there are bats, there are caves."

They found the mouth of the cave just beyond the break in the trees. They built a campfire under a rock overhang on flat stones that were perfect for sleeping. Beyond the campsite, the cave narrowed. They knew not to go any farther in. Even though the bats were gone for the night, they didn't want to be caught inside the cave when the bats returned in the morning.

Kim had brought a package of hot dogs. They each slid one onto a stick and roasted it over the fire while they discussed the day's adventures. Somewhere during the hike up to the rocks, Kimo had realized that the lava flow in Gasper's Gulch meant there might not be any wizzleroaches nearby. "They have to be gone, right? I mean, they used to live in the gulch and now it's full of rock."

"They probably flew off when they felt the

heat of the molten lava coming down the mountain," said Kim.

"I kinda feel bad for them," Pippa offered. She was always taking the side of helpless creatures—even wizzleroaches.

But Kimo could not feel bad. He slid his cooked hot dog off the stick and tore it in half with his teeth. "I might get to like this house," he said. "Now that the roaches are gone."

"We haven't found the house yet," said Pippa, though she had begun to let herself imagine that they might, because if they did, she would have a place to hang her knickknack shelf. What would I collect if I had a place to put my collection? the little girl thought.

For Kim, who loved books, there was something perfectly poetically right about finding a house because of a hint in a book. "We will find it," she said. "I'm sure of it."

Pippa rolled her eyes. "You were sure we'd get there before dark."

Kim ignored this. She had already eaten her dinner and was lying on a flat stone with her head resting on her backpack. She had a flashlight propped up under her chin and was reading from the textbook. "It says here Captain Baker lived in the house for twenty-five years. He had a garden of rare orchids and a pond where he kept fish."

"Hmm," murmured Toby, clutching the jar that held his own fish a little tighter.

"He collected rare books and scrimshaw."

"What's scrimshaw?" asked Pippa, thinking about her knickknack shelf.

"No idea," said Kimo.

Kim picked up reading again. "Captain Baker used to take his baths in the pool beneath the waterfall. And he threw parties whenever there was a full moon. He invited musicians from all over the island. There was dancing and singing. And one night, Captain Baker . . ." Kim trailed off. She'd read a little ahead and what she'd read had alarmed her.

"What?" asked Pippa. "One night . . . what?"

"Nothing," said Kim, snapping the textbook closed and turning off the flashlight.

"What does it say?" Pippa's eyes were narrowed with suspicion.

"Nothing," said Kim. "I think I should save the batteries."

"Give me that," said Pippa, reaching for the book.

But Kim held it close to her chest. "No," she said. "You can look at it later."

"You're being weird," said Kimo.

"Totally," echoed Toby.

Before Kim could deny it, the baby began to cry and point at the backpack where her bottle was kept. "You want a bottle?" Kim slid one out of the pack. "Come and get it." She held it out to Penny, hoping the baby would crawl to her, but Penny, who was sitting in Kimo's lap, didn't move.

"Should we be worried?" asked Pippa. "I mean, how old was I when I crawled?"

"About the same age as Penny," Kim said, relieved that they had all moved of the subject of the textbook, which she now slid into her backpack.

She didn't want any of them to read the words that she had read: silly words, full of superstition. If she were to share those words, her siblings would want to turn around and head back down the hill and never look for Captain Baker's house again, because the words said that one night, at one of his parties, Captain Baker had slipped on an orchid petal, hit his head, and died. But he wasn't entirely gone; since then, his ghost was said to have been seen roaming the forests of Mount Muldoon.

That night, while the others slept, Kim Fitzgerald-Trout did something she had never done before. She defaced her school textbook. "I'm so sorry," she whispered as she slowly and methodically tore the offending page from the book. "It has to be done." She crumpled up the paper and placed it on the dying embers of the campfire. Later Kim told me that if anyone had been able to see her face in the dark, they would have seen how guilty she looked as she watched the piece of paper catch fire.

From where she lay, Kim could see—just beyond the stone overhang—the full moon. Was it possible Captain Baker's ghost was roaming the hills, even now? She didn't believe in ghosts. She thought the very idea was ridiculous. But she knew her siblings would not feel the same way. They would not move into a house on a mountain if the house and the mountain were haunted.

The next morning as they packed up their campsite, Pippa and Kimo argued about which direction they should hike in order to find the waterfall. Now that the path was obscured by the hardened black lava, there was no clear route. But Pippa was sure she knew which way to go. The problem was that Kimo was equally sure that he knew, and he was pointing in the opposite direction. Things were uncharacteristically tense between them and it didn't help that they'd all had only one tube of crackers and a couple of sticks of beef jerky to share for breakfast.

While Pippa and Kimo argued and Toby stood watching them in silence (with his arms crossed over his grumbling stomach), Kim hoisted the baby onto her hip and started off toward the quiet of the trees. She was hoping that the hoots of early morning owls returning home to their nests would drown out the grouchy snarls of her siblings, but what happened was even better.

As she stepped into the woods, she looked up toward the treetops and was surprised to see a sprig of bright purple flowers growing from the trunk of one of the trees. An orchid, she thought. That's rare. Then she saw another spray of purple erupting from another tree trunk, and then another, and another.

"They're everywhere," she said to the baby, setting her down on the ground between two ferns and stepping closer to the orchids. She saw that if she squinted, the orchids formed a trail of purple leading into the woods, and that's when she remembered the passage that she'd read the night before—the passage that said Captain Baker had planted a garden full of orchids. Was it possible that these orchids were descended from Captain Baker's? Was it possible that they had grown in the garden and spread to other parts of the forest? If so, then it was possible that if she followed the purple flowers, they would lead to Captain Baker's garden . . . and his house.

She turned and ran out of the woods, shouting to the others, "Hey, I know how to find it!"

After half an hour of following the purple flowers, the children found themselves at the edge of the wood, looking out over a bright, open clearing filled with thousands of orchids swaying like elegant, bright dancers in the breeze. Across the clearing, beyond the sea of purple, there was an even stranger sight: an enormous leafy green structure.

"It's the house," Kim gasped.

"Not unless the house is made of salad," Kimo challenged.

"I hate salad," offered Toby.

Pippa didn't take a side. She was already moving around the edge of the woods to take in the view. The others followed her. As they cleared the tree line, they could see down the mountain. On their right was the Bay of Hanalee, where enormous ships plied the waters. Across the ravine on their left rose the mist above the waterfall at Makapepe. And if they looked down over the tops of the trees that grew on the lower part of the mountain, they could just make out, far below them, a garbage truck driving the road toward the marsh at the edge of the Sakahatchi. "This is Captain Baker's view," Pippa concluded.

We've done it, Kim thought. We've found the house—even Pippa agrees. Kim started toward the green structure. As she got closer, the salad of green resolved itself into distinct vines and plants that had taken root in the old lava walls.

Low-slung bushes and trees grew around the outside, but between them there was a stone path that led toward a gap in the green where the front door had once been. The wooden door had long ago rotted away and in its place there was nothing now but a spider's web that glittered in the morning sunlight. Without saying a word, they all ducked low under the web and entered the structure.

What they saw on the other side of the web took their breath away.

Anything that had been made of wood had long ago vanished, swallowed by the forest and the rains, so there were no divisions now—no walls, no ceilings, no floors. Instead of floorboards, the ground was thick with moss that felt like a soft and spongy carpet. There was no roof, and any glass that had once been in the window frames was gone too, broken by time or weather. Where the windows had once been, there were openings in the stone with tree branches poking through and long curtains of vines. And everywhere the children looked were the bright colors of orchids and bromeliads blooming from the volcanic rock.

The whole place was more like a great green cathedral than a house, and the children treated it that way, standing silently, like you would in a church or a mosque or a synagogue. The air was filled with birdsong. A swallow flew out of its nest and swooped up toward the sky, maneuvering past a tall column of stone. "Is that a fireplace?" Kim asked, following the bird's path with her eye.

"They're all over the place," Kimo answered. He quickly counted. "There are eleven down on the ground. Look how the others are on top of them—up in the air." It was true. The fireplaces had been built in each of the rooms on each of the three stories of the house. Now that the walls and ceilings were gone, the fireplaces were the only way that you would know the house had once been three stories tall. From each ground-floor fireplace a chimney sprouted and above that chimney—ten or twelve feet up—was another fireplace (that had once been on the second floor) and above that— sprouting from another section of the chimney— was a third fireplace (that had once been on the third floor) and above that sprouted the last section of the chimney, the part that had once poked out of the roof.

"Thirty-three fireplaces all together," gasped Pippa.

"There were thirty-three rooms," said Kim. "The book was right." And she felt a twinge of guilt thinking of how she'd ruined the book by burning one of its pages. Then she thought about that page and the story of Captain Baker's ghost;

she was very glad not to be trying to convince her siblings that it was just a story. Better that they don't know, she thought. Better that they never, ever know. She turned to look at Pippa, who was smiling. "You have a place to put your knickknack shelf," said Kim.

Pippa was thinking the same thing. But she hated to give her older sister too much satisfaction, so she just said, "It's hard to hang a shelf on a wall made of stone."

"You'll figure out a way," said Kim, just as Kimo poked her in the ribs.

"Good job," he said. "I'm glad you were paying attention in history class. Otherwise, we'd never have found this place." The oldest two children shared a smile.

"Quit it," said Pippa, turning to glare at Toby, who was staring at her. "Don't look at me like that."

"Goldie wants to tell you something," the boy said, holding up the jar.

"I can't read his mind," Pippa said with a snort.

"I know," said Toby. "Only I can do that. Here's his message. He says: '*Oo-ooh, aa-aah*.'"

"What does that mean?" Pippa stared at him blankly.

Toby elbowed her in the side. "*Oo-ooh, aa-aah*," he said. "Come on. Goldie's saying that you lost the bet."

Kimo laughed. "This is the house. You did say you'd be a monkey's uncle if we found it. Better act like one."

Pippa scowled, then robotically said, "*Oo-ooh, aa-aah*."

"Put a little feeling into it," said Kim, pulling out a bottle of water from the backpack and passing it around.

"*Oo-ooh, aa-aah*," Pippa sighed.

"Don't just say it," said Kimo. "Do it." Pippa didn't say anything. "You gave your word."

Like all Fitzgerald-Trouts, Pippa believed that giving your word was sacred. So she complied, lifting her arm, scratching under her armpit, and saying, "*Oo-ooh, aa-aah.*"

"That's better," said Kim.

"You said you'd do it till we tell you to stop," Toby reminded her.

Pippa stuck her tongue out but said, "*Oo-ooh, aa-aah. Oo-ooh, aa-aah. Oo-ooh, aa-aah.*" She looked at them, but no one told her to stop. She narrowed her eyes. "You are going to want me to stop. Believe me, you are going to be begging."

She began to chant, "*Oo-ooh, aa-aah,*" over and over, very loudly, scratching her armpits and dancing like a monkey. She even grabbed one of the vines that hung from a branch that grew through a window. "*Oo-ooh, aa-aah,*" she shrieked as she took hold of the vine, scrambled up onto the window opening, and launched herself into the air, swinging out over the room. When she was at the highest point, she let go, dropping down and falling onto the soft moss in a position that knocked her glasses off. She felt around in the moss until her fingers found them and she could put them back on. Then she looked at her siblings expectantly, but none of them told her to stop.

Instead, Kimo grabbed the vine, climbing up just as Pippa had and swinging out over the room too. Toby was the next to try it, launching himself off the window and giggling with joy as he let go of the vine and fell through the air. Then Kim took a turn.

They went on like this, taking turns swinging on the vines, and all the while Pippa was shouting, "*Oo-ooh, aa-aah,*" and dancing like a monkey. But no one was really watching her anymore and they certainly weren't telling her to stop; they were busy swinging from vines—or in Penny's case, rolling around on the soft green moss and playing with her own two feet.

"Come on," Pippa said. "Enough is enough. Let me stop." But the others paid no attention. "Fine," she said, and twirled off across the room, shouting,

"*Oo-ooh, aa-aah,*" even louder and scratching under her armpits even more ferociously. She ducked out of the house. If I'm a monkey, I should be in the jungle, she was thinking as she *Oo-ooh-aa-aah*-ed at the top of her lungs and bobbed between the trunks of trees. She spun and jumped and scratched and shouted until she was so out of breath and dizzy that she stumbled and bumped against one of the tree trunks.

From inside the house, the others heard the thump and came running to see what had happened. They found Pippa under the tree, holding her sore shoulder and laughing.

"What's so funny?" Kim asked.

Pippa pointed up at an enormous bunch of ripe yellow bananas that swayed over her head. "*Oo-ooh, aa-aah,*" she deadpanned.

"You found lunch," Kim said. "I think you deserve to be able to stop the monkey noises now." She looked to Toby for his agreement since he was the one who'd made the bet.

Toby nodded solemnly, then said, "Let's eat."

But they didn't eat right away. Instead they did a very un-monkeylike thing. They built a fire in one of the fireplaces and they fried slices of bananas on the hot volcanic stone. Kim found a packet of hot chocolate mix crammed in the corner of the backpack and sprinkled it on the bananas to give them an extra-sweet flavor. Maybe it was their excitement about the house or maybe it was their hunger, but the Fitzgerald-Trouts all agreed it was the best thing any of them had ever tasted.

For the rest of the day, the Fitzgerald-Trouts worked to make the Castle (as they had taken to calling it) feel like home. The first order of business was to construct a roof. After all, a house was only a house if it could keep out the rain. They lay on their backs beside one of the fireplaces, staring up at the canopy of trees and trying to imagine how a roof would ever materialize. Toby suggested that they put wood or tree branches across the space, but Pippa scoffed at this. She knew enough from woodworking class to know that the space was so enormous they would never find wood beams long enough—nor would they be able to lift them into place.

"You got a better idea?" Toby challenged.

"Maybe," said Pippa, lapsing into silence for a moment and looking over at the doorway where the spider sat on its glistening web. Some creatures build their homes in the air, she thought. Then she said, "What if the roof weren't made of wood . . . what if it were strung up like a web?"

"Strung up with what?"

Pippa remembered that at the wharf where they'd once docked their boat, the friendly dockmaster, Oshiro, let people leave old sails that didn't pass the test for sailing (they were too stretched) so that others could take them and use them as tarps and boat covers. "What if we used those sails that Oshiro gives away?" she said.

The Fitzgerald-Trouts lost no time in hiking down the mountain and driving to the wharf, where they talked to Oshiro. Not only did he let them have the sails, but he helped them pile as many as they could into the trunk of the little green car. After that, they decided to make a stop for food. They'd found their monthly envelope of grocery money from Tina in the glove compartment of the car a few days before.

While they were at the store, they ran into their favorite clerk, Asha, who was working at the checkout counter. Some months before, they had helped Asha straighten out a romantic misunderstanding with her boyfriend, the owner of the nearby laundromat, Mr. Knuckles. Once the confusion was resolved, Asha and Mr. Knuckles had decided to get married. Ever since then, whenever Asha ran into the Fitzgerald-Trouts, she gave them free day-old doughnuts.

Now they found themselves standing at the cash register, listening to Asha describe the renovations she was doing to the apartment she and Mr. Knuckles lived in above his laundromat. Asha was one of the children's favorite grown-ups. But even she could not make a story about apartment renovations interesting, especially when the children were thinking about renovations to their own new leafy residence. They were relieved when another customer appeared and they could make a quick exit, taking the bag of old doughnuts that Asha had offered them.

They ate the doughnuts right away, along with some apples and some pieces of Island Belle cheese. They loved this cheese because each circular piece came wrapped in red wax, and after pulling the wax off, they could mold it into big, fake red lips that stuck to their faces. They were just finishing their wax creations as Kim pulled into the Muldoon Park Parking Lot.

Wearing their fake lips, the children lugged the sails (and the groceries) up the mountain to the Castle. Kimo did most of the carrying—in fact, he did two trips while the others only made one—but he was happy about it because he'd decided that running up and down the trail carrying a heavy sail on his back was good weekend training for the pole vault. Besides, they'd found a quicker route to the house across the hardened lava at Gasper's Gulch, and the trip between the parking lot and the car took them less than half an hour.

Once they were all back at the Castle, the children (led by Pippa) tied ropes to each of the sails' corners, and then crawled up the fireplaces and lashed the ropes around the chimneys so that the sails were stretched out and hung overhead like waterproof tarps. Now they really did have a home. But they hadn't spent a night in it yet, and they had no idea what was coming.

CHAPTER

5

As the sun began to set, the Fitzgerald-Trouts began to prepare their first dinner in the Castle. They'd brought a few pots and pans for cooking, and while Kimo heated up an extra-large can of beef stew, Kim made corn bread. Kim loved to bake, and for her, one of the most wonderful things about the Castle was that it had a little square space above the kitchen fire-place with a metal door that could be bolted shut. Kim wasn't sure how well it would hold heat, and even if it did she knew the temperature would be erratic, but she decided to try baking something anyway. She stirred a corn-bread mix in a bowl and then poured it into a cast-iron skillet. She set the skillet inside the fireplace-oven and waited, hoping against hope that the bread would bake. It took almost an hour, but at the end of the hour there was hot corn bread. Kim cut it like a pie and squeezed honey onto the wedges, and they ate it with the stew.

After dinner, Kimo made hot chocolate and they all raised their mugs, offering a toast to the spider who had inspired their roof, then slurped their drinks appreciatively. It was only after their mugs were empty that they realized they had no way to wash the dishes. It was a small crisis. How would they live in a real house if they couldn't wash dishes? And this raised the even bigger question: if they couldn't wash dishes, how would they wash themselves? When they'd camped at the beach, they'd always bathed in the ocean or in the public showers. But now what would they do?

It was Kimo who solved the problem. "The waterfall," he said.

They all knew the waterfall at Makapepe. Over the years, they'd hiked to it, picking the guavas that grew around its edges and swimming in the big pool beneath it. But how to get to the waterfall from here?

"You know who would know?" Pippa mused.

And Kim almost said, "The ghost of Captain Baker?" All day long she'd been thinking about the burned page in the book and wondering if she should tell the others. Now that they all loved the Castle, maybe they wouldn't abandon it. Maybe they would agree with her that ghosts didn't exist and ghost stories were ridiculous.

"The deer," Pippa said before Kim could decide whether to speak. "I've seen deer trails all over the mountain. There's one from here, heading down into the ravine."

"The waterfall's across the ravine," Toby said.

"Duh," said Pippa. "That's what I mean."

"You're mean," he said and pulled her hair. They might have gotten into a full-blown fight, but the baby started to cry, bringing them back to their better selves.

"Let's go," said Kimo and Kim in unison.

Carrying flashlights and a cooler full of dirty dishes, they followed the deer trail down into the ravine and within a few minutes they could hear the roar of the waterfall. They stumbled out of the trees and found themselves at the edge of the pool. They knew it well, but they had never seen it in moonlight, when it took on a fairy-tale quality. Or maybe not a fairy tale, thought Kim. What if this is the beginning of a ghost story? Should I say something? She squelched the thought. The roar of the waterfall is so loud they won't be able to hear me anyway.

Besides, her brothers and sisters were already charging into the water in their clothes. Pippa was carrying Penny. She pulled the baby's diaper off, tossing it onto the rocks before she lowered herself and Penny into the water.

"Coooo!" Penny shrieked, which Pippa thought probably meant that the water was cold (which it was). But a second later, it felt just right, and she and the baby waded deeper into the pond, heading toward the waterfall. They stood just on the edge of the downpour, where it wasn't too strong, and the water splashed over them as gently as raindrops.

Kimo had the cooler of dishes floating beside him. Standing up to his waist in water, he scrubbed the dirty dishes with the dark mud and grit at the edge of the pond. He was careful to clean the dishes downstream from the others so that the water washed the debris away.

When both the dishes and the Fitzgerald-Trouts were clean, the children drifted into the middle of the pond, staring up at the stars. The roar of the waterfall now seemed to be coming from the sky itself, almost as if all of the stars were in motion, thundering toward them.

Inspired by the noise, Kimo hollered, "Give a loud shout 'cause we're Fitzgerald-Trouts. We don't give up and we don't give in . . ."

Before he could try a verse, Kim triumphantly sang, "We live in a castle on a mountain!"

"We find a pond and start to swim," Pippa offered.

"We get a house and we name it Tim!" proclaimed Toby. Everyone looked at him. He'd made possibly the most ridiculous rhyme ever.

Kimo laughed and continued the song. "And now we start all over again . . ."

They went on chanting and making up verses

as they waded out of the pool and started toward their new home.

After a long day spent making roofs and cooking and swimming, the children quickly fell asleep in a large heap beside the kitchen fireplace. With the moss under them and the sail-roof high above, they felt sheltered and safe. So it was completely unexpected when, several hours later, they heard a strange and sinister noise that shook the branches of the trees. They all sat bolt upright, terrified.

"What was that?" Kimo whispered.

"No idea." This was Pippa, who was holding onto the baby (the only one still asleep). "Something rustling," she said. Then she added, "And slurping." Even as she said the word *slurping*, she felt a chill up her spine. How could something living on a mountain slurp?

"Slurping," said Kimo. "What could be slurping?" He looked at Kim, but Kim was looking away. She couldn't face Kimo. She was thinking of the page she'd burned from the textbook, and the secret she was keeping.

"I think it's . . ." Toby trailed off. What he was thinking was so awful that he couldn't say it unless he knew for sure. He lifted up Goldie's jar in the moonlight. Goldie's eyes told him that Goldie was thinking the same thing. "Ghost," Toby said in the quietest whisper.

Kim shuddered at the mention of a ghost, but then she reasoned with herself and said, "It must have been the trees."

"Trees rustle," said Pippa. "But they don't slurp or squelch or whatever that sound is."

"Shh," Kimo said. "I think I hear it again . . ." They all huddled closer together with their arms around each other and listened with all of their might.

Sqq-sqq, tss-tss. Sqq-sqq, tss-tss. There it was. The rustle and the slurp—only this time it sounded even closer, a few yards beyond the Castle's walls.

"See . . ." said Toby. "Ghost."

"Maybe not," said Kimo.

"What, then?" hissed Pippa, who had drawn the same conclusion as Toby.

"A monster," Kimo offered, comforting no one.

"Should we run?" This was Toby.

Kim squeezed closer to her brothers and sisters. "Better stay still. Maybe it doesn't know we're here."

"What if it does?" Toby asked.

"Shhh . . ." They crouched together in silence, thankful that the baby was asleep, and waited with wildly beating hearts. The rustle and the slurp got closer and closer till it seemed the ghost or monster or whatever it was was just on the other side of the Castle's wall.

For Kim, each of these long seconds was like a pain in her heart because she knew she was holding on to the terrible secret of Captain Baker's ghost.

But there it was, the sound: *Tss-tss. Tss-tss. Tss-tss. Tss-tss.*

They all realized at the same moment that they were only hearing the rustling now. The slurping had stopped. They looked at each other, exchanging this knowledge and the added information that the rustling came from up high, near the top of the tree that branched through the open window.

It's above us, Toby thought. And this was more than he could contain. He opened his mouth, letting out a howl of terror. "Aaaaaaaaaah!"

"Quiet, Toby!" Pippa shouted at the same moment that Kimo barked, "Stop yelling." They all screamed at each other for several minutes, anticipating that the ghost or monster or whatever it was would swoop down through the window and eat them up or do whatever it is that ghosts and monsters do.

Only nothing happened.

They fell silent. The baby, who'd been woken up by the screaming, cried out and reached for her octopus while the older children waited nervously for the next sound. But the rustling had stopped. The trees beyond the Castle were quiet. Whatever had been there was gone, chased away by their noise. They lay back down and moved in closer together, shutting their eyes and trying to forget what had happened. Kim lay awake the longest, arguing with herself. Should she keep the secret of Captain Baker's ghost? It seemed deceitful not to tell the others now that they had heard such frightening noises, and yet if she told her siblings, they might force her to abandon the Castle—something she was not willing to do. No ghost is going to scare us away from our home, she thought. Besides, it can't be a ghost. There's no such thing as ghosts.

But something had made the terrifying sounds. And if it wasn't a ghost, what was it?

CHAPTER
6

When they woke up on Sunday morning, they were surprisingly well rested. Thanks to the comfortable moss and the relative darkness of the Castle (with its high walls and thick canopy of trees), the sun didn't wake them until much later than usual, so they'd all managed to get a good night's sleep. One by one they stood up and stretched, talking in quiet voices as they rekindled the cooking fire. "I feel like a million bucks," Kimo said. "If only

Ms. Bonicle were around today, I bet I'd break that record."

By the time they were sitting around the fireplace drinking hot chocolate, they all agreed that they loved their new home so much they would not let whatever had made the terrible noise frighten them away.

"But we need to protect ourselves," said Pippa.

"How?" asked Kimo.

"I bet Goldie knows," said Toby, who was staring into the fish's jar.

"Why would a fish know?" This was Pippa again.

"Animals know things," said Toby. "Remember how before a volcano erupts all the birds fly out of the trees?"

"The noise did sound like it came from an animal," offered Kim, who didn't think it had sounded like that at all. But it can't be a ghost, she thought. I don't believe in ghosts.

"We all agree that we shouldn't be frightened," said Kimo. "We like this house too much to leave. And besides, whatever it is, it left us alone."

They all nodded and took sips of their hot chocolate. Then Pippa floated a question. "What if it wasn't one thing making that noise . . . what if it was *two* things?"

"Two?!" Toby shouted.

"We just agreed we wouldn't be scared." Kimo glared at Pippa. "Now you're scaring everyone."

"I'm just saying," Pippa mused, "there was a rustling sound and a slurping sound, but the slurping sound stopped before the rustling sound, so maybe they were made by two different things."

"I get it," Kim said. "In that case we can take care of them separately. For the rustle, well, we already know what to do. We make a lot of noise. That's what scared it off last night."

"So maybe we make a bunch of alarms," Pippa said. "Like we fill soda pop cans with rocks and hang them in all the windows and in the doorway. That way if the rustling thing tries to come into the house, it bumps into one of the cans and gets scared off."

Kimo smiled at his little sister. "Makes sense." He loved her knack for invention.

"The slurping sound came from down low," Pippa continued. "So for the slurp, we need to avoid being close to the ground."

"Hammocks," said Kim. "We use the rest of the old sails to make hammocks."

"Great idea." Kimo surveyed the space. "There are enough tree branches coming through the windows that there'll be plenty of places to hang them."

"And they're comfy. Maybe even comfier than sleeping on moss," Kim said.

"I told you fish know things," said Toby, who had been staring at Goldie.

"What are you talking about?" Pippa yanked on Toby's ear. "I'm the one who solved the problem."

Toby shoved Pippa in return. "Quit it! You're always so mean."

"And you're always making stuff up!"

"I'm not making stuff up," said Toby. "Just because *you* can't tell what Goldie's thinking doesn't mean that *I* can't."

"Oh, please!"

"I'm staying as far away from you as I can!" the boy shouted, shoving Goldie's jar into Kim's hands and racing off.

Kim and Kimo shared a look, then Kim turned to Pippa. "Why can't you be nice?"

"Because I tell the truth," Pippa said defensively. "And the truth isn't always nice." She wasn't going to admit it, but she always felt rotten after she'd fought with her little brother.

"Can't you *think* the truth but not *say* it out loud?" Kim lifted up the goldfish jar and peered into it, talking to the fish. "Should we follow him?" She was kidding; she didn't really think the fish could tell her whether to follow Toby.

"He isn't going far," said Kimo. "If he was, he would have taken Goldie with him."

Kimo was right. A minute later Toby climbed back through the window. He was holding an armful of sticks.

"What ya doing, Tobes?" Kimo asked in a syrupy voice.

"These sticks mark my room." Toby started laying out the sticks on the ground to mark a corner of the Castle. "They're like a wall. Kim, Kimo, you can come in any time you want. But you," he turned to stare daggers at Pippa, "can't ever come in."

"Fine," said Pippa. "I'll make a room of my own."

"Whatever," said Toby. "Just don't come into mine!"

A few minutes later, they had all chosen a room and marked it with a line of sticks. Kim had decided to make hers near the kitchen fireplace so she could practice baking without disturbing the others.

Once Toby had chosen his corner of the room and built his line of sticks, the baby reached her arms up to him, making clear that she wanted to go wherever he was. Pippa felt a sharp pain in her heart. She'd always been the one who took the most care of Penny, and it hurt now to see the baby so fond of Toby instead. She took her hurt feelings off to the woods, saying that she would gather small rocks to make the soda can alarms. As soon as she'd left, Toby rigged Penny a small hammock beside his own. Kim and Kimo set off down the mountain to get more sailcloth at the wharf. Toby was left alone with the baby.

Later, the Fitzgerald-Trout children would say that this was the moment that things began to change between them. They would tell me that because the Castle and the mountain allowed them more freedom, they each began to pay less attention to what the whole group needed and more attention to what each of them, alone, wanted.

"The terrible thing that happened to us didn't happen for weeks, but that day was important," Kim said. "With Kimo and me down at the wharf, Toby and Penny back at the Castle, and

Pippa searching for rocks to make the soda pop alarms."

In fact, Pippa wasn't searching for rocks. That was what she'd said she was going to do, but instead she was eating the guavas from the trees that grew near the pond and listening to the water-fall roaring beside her. It was a noise that appealed to her, in the same way the sound of the saw bit-ing down into wood appealed to her. Both sounds reminded her of how she felt on the inside a lot of time. *Angry.*

She opened her mouth and let out a giant roar, a sound to compete with the waterfall. But what am I mad about? she wondered. Then she thought: maybe I'm not mad, maybe I'm hurt. Even as this occurred to her, the waterfall unleashed a log that flew past her and knocked one of the larger rocks beside her into the water. Her heart hammered in her chest. It was such a close call; another cou-ple of inches and the log would have hit her in the head.

She looked down at the rock that had fallen in the water. It was as big as a coconut, and it had been knocked loose from its spot on the shore. She lifted it up, thinking that she would set it back into place, but as she did, she caught a glimpse of something bright and white. Setting the rock back down, she picked up the white object and inspected it.

It was a polished bone the size of her hand. One side was blank, but on the other side someone had used a thin knife to carve the image of a three-masted sailing ship. In her years of searching the beach for glass and shells, she had found many interesting things, but she had never found anything so special and so rare. She had never found a piece of art. And I found it by accident, she thought. I wasn't even looking. Even stranger, she realized that it didn't belong to anyone, which meant that it now belonged to her.

She tried to remember the last time that she had owned anything special. Anything that was hers alone. Sure, she had a sleeping bag and she had clothes. She had a school backpack, and she had binders filled with lined paper, and she had notebooks. But those weren't special things. The last special thing that she'd had was her doll, Lani. But as soon as Penny had come along, the doll had become the baby's.

This is mine, Pippa thought. And not only is it the most beautiful thing I've ever owned, it's the most beautiful thing in the world. Then she thought about her knickknack shelf. As soon as she finished building it, she would find a way to hang it from the wall of her room—her own special and separate space in the Castle—and she would set the piece of bone on it.

When she returned from the pond with a backpack full of pebbles and the piece of bone in her pocket, Kimo and Kim were there, back from their trip to the wharf and the grocery store. They were sitting on the moss in the middle of Kim's part of the Castle, turning the old sails into hammocks and drinking cans of Uncle Ozo's soda pop. Toby smiled apologetically at Pippa and held out a can. "Here," he said. "We have to drink it to make the—" But before Toby could finish saying that they needed to drink the soda pop so that the cans would be empty to make the rock alarms, he let out a long, loud burp. Kim and Kimo opened their mouths to laugh at Toby's burp, but burps came out of them too. Uncle Ozo's had twice the bubbles of other soda pops, which meant that it made anyone who drank it burp. Not wanting to be left out of the fun, Pippa grabbed a can, cracked it open, and swallowed half of the doubly bubbly stuff in one gulp.

Soon all the older Fitzgerald-Trouts were burping, which made them laugh, which made them burp more, which made them laugh more. It was a terribly wonderful cycle—or a wonderfully terrible cycle, depending on how you looked at it. They rolled around on the ground, clutching their bellies, sore from all the burping and all the laughter. The baby, who was too young to drink soda pop, sat at a distance, holding onto her octopus and staring at her older siblings with unblinking eyes. If anyone had happened to stumble upon the Fitzgerald-Trouts, they would have thought them a joyful and carefree bunch. They would not have seen the tiny cracks that were starting to grow between them. But the cracks were there.

CHAPTER

7

The children woke early on Monday morning while it was still dark in the Castle. They ate a quick breakfast, packed their backpacks, and headed single file down the hill, with Kimo carrying Penny. They sang as they went, "Give a loud shout 'cause we're Fitzgerald-Trouts . . ." And fifteen minutes later, they were in the parking lot at the base of Mount Muldoon.

The sun glared off the windshield, blinding Kim as she climbed into the driver's seat. Someday I'll find a pair of sunglasses, she thought, and then she had the completely unrelated thought that it had been so dark when they'd left the Castle that she'd gathered her things without being able to see them and had left her history book lying in the moss beneath her hammock. It was strange to realize that now that they had a house, they could forget things. That had certainly never happened when they'd lived in the car and carried all their possessions with them wherever they went. Oh well, thought Kim. It's worth it. I'd rather have a house and forget things every once in a while then live in a car. But then she realized that not only had she forgotten the book, she had forgotten to study for her history test, the test on chapters five and six that was the first thing on her schedule that morning.

"Do I have time to run back up to the Castle?"

"No," the others chorused. "We'll be late."

"I didn't study history." Kim's voice wavered with emotion. "It's an oral test. I'm going to have to say my answers out loud."

"You'll do fine," said Kimo, patting Kim on the shoulder. "You always do." Kim took a deep breath and forced herself to smile. Kimo was right. She usually did do fine. She'd never gotten a grade lower than a B-plus. So what if she got a B or a B-minus? It wouldn't be the end of the world.

"Okay," she said. "Everybody buckled up? Let's go."

F. That was the letter on the grade sheet for Kim's history test. F.

"F is for *failure*," Kim said, fighting the feeling that she was going to cry. Around them the other schoolchildren were running and laughing, enjoying their recess. But not the Fitzgerald-Trouts—they were trying to comfort Kim.

Pippa had never seen her older sister so upset before. "It's just a grade," she said.

"But I didn't get one single question right," said Kim. "I just stood there and I didn't know the answers and I . . . I just moved my mouth up and down, like I was a goldfish gulping water."

"That sounds nice," said Toby.

"It wasn't," said Kim, swatting at her eyes. "Everyone was laughing."

"Are you crying?" Pippa asked.

"No." Kim straightened up defensively.

"You'll make it up next time," said Kimo. Kim turned and stared at him. For the first time in her life, she felt how unfair it was that they were only a few months apart in age but that he was in a lower grade. Kimo got to enjoy sixth grade while Kim suffered through seventh.

"Now you're just like the rest of us," said Pippa, who had actually never gotten an F before and was mildly impressed by her older sister's failure.

"F is for fart," said Toby with a snort. They all laughed, and Kim felt a little better.

"Mr. Petty says I have to stay after school for something called 'test corrections.'"

"That's when you sit and write out the right

answers," said Kimo, who knew something about getting grades that weren't As.

"But it was an oral test."

"He probably wants to make sure you know everything," Kimo said. "They give you questions and you can use the textbook."

"Why don't they just do that to begin with?" asked Pippa.

It was such a good question that no one could answer it, so Kim said, "Hope you guys don't mind waiting for me." None of them did. Pippa knew the woodworking shop would be open and was excited to finish her knickknack shelf, and Kimo was happy to put in the time at the track working on the pole vault. Kimo knew that the more he practiced, the more likely he was to break the record. He smiled to himself, thinking about his father, Johnny Trout, opening the newspaper and seeing the news of Kimo's accomplishment. Johnny might feel proud enough to let the children take back the fishing boat.

Kim turned to Toby. "Tobes, can you get Penny from day care and hang out with her on the playground? She likes being with you best these days."

"Yeah, sure," Toby said, feeling proud to be the designated babysitter.

So it was that that afternoon Toby found himself lying in the grass watching the baby tug at dandelions, using her little fists to make them explode. If he looked to his left, he could see—far off across the field—the classroom where Kim was doing her test corrections. If he looked to his right, he could see the entrance to the track where at that very moment Kimo was planting the pole in the pit and launching

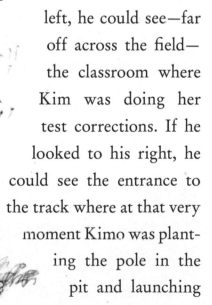

himself up into the air. It isn't fair that Kimo gets to break an island record, Toby thought. I want to break a record.

But what record?

He began to make a list of the things that he was good at. He looked over at Goldie in his jar in the grass. I'm good at taking care of a goldfish, he thought. And I'm good at taking care of babies. But on second thought he realized those weren't the kinds of things that counted toward an island record. What else was he good at?

He was good at chewing gum. In fact, he remembered a time when Pippa—Pippa, who was so hard to impress!—had been amazed that he'd been able to cram all twenty-four sticks from a pack of gum into his mouth at once. And now that he thought about it, he realized that there had been room for more. If he'd had another pack, he would have put that in his mouth too. I wonder if there's an island record for chewing the most gum? But then he thought about how he would have to convince Kim and Kimo to let him buy a lot of gum, and Pippa was sure to hear about it, and she would probably try it too, and Pippa had a very big mouth.

There must be something else. What about fingernails? Toby knew for a fact that his fingernails were longer than anyone else's in his class. And Kim had often said—when she was trying to get him to cut them—that they were the longest nails she had ever seen. What if there was a record for longest fingernails? If there was, didn't Toby have a chance of winning? Maybe not now, but if he let his fingernails grow for a while. Then he thought about how long it would take. If I try to break the record, it probably won't happen until I'm a grown-up. And this thought—that he might someday be a grown-up—was so awful to Toby that he groaned out loud. "Ugh."

"Ugh what?"

He turned and found Clarice McGuffin sitting in the backseat of her limousine, staring at him through the open window. When had the limo pulled up and how long had she been watching?

"Ugh what?" she asked again, pushing a loose strand of hair back with her finger.

Toby saw that her fingernails were much, much longer than his. Of course they are, he thought. She's probably been growing them since she was my age. But he didn't say this. "Ugh nothing," he said, then added, "Why are you here?"

"Good," Clarice said. "Getting right to the point. I like that."

"Wimo," said Penny. She had stopped playing with the dandelions and was pointing at Clarice. "Wimo."

"How precious." Clarice smiled her tight-lipped smile. "She likes me."

Toby hadn't forgotten all the things his siblings had said about Clarice. "It's your car she likes," he said gruffly.

"Perhaps she wants a ride," said Clarice.

"Is that what *you* want?" asked Toby. "Because you haven't answered my question."

"You're right," said Clarice. "The truth is that my company . . ."

"Baby Loves," Toby interrupted. "You're the President and CEO—whatever that is."

Clarice looked a little surprised. "That's right," she said. "Baby Loves is having a contest."

"I love contests," said Toby, smiling down at Goldie. He had won the goldfish in a contest at the laundromat.

"I know you do," said Clarice. "That's why I think you should enter this one. There's only one catch. You can't enter the contest without a baby."

"I have a baby," Toby said matter-of-factly, and as if on cue, Penny reached out her arms to him. The boy scooped her up and pulled her close. "What do you think," he asked the baby, "Do you want to enter a contest?"

Bang! Bang! Bang! Pippa drove the nail down into the wood, hammering together the pieces of her knickknack shelf. Each time a nail was hammered in, she took another nail from her pocket and positioned its tip on the wood, then raised her arm and brought the hammer down. *Bang! Bang! Bang!*

Occasionally as she worked, she looked over at the image of the three-masted sailing ship. She had set the piece of carved bone on the workbench as inspiration since she was building the shelf to hold it. Even so, when Bronco Bragg came over, gestured to the bone, and gave a long, low whistle of appreciation, Pippa was surprised. She had forgotten that anyone else could see it.

"Quite a beaut," he said. He was chewing on a long piece of dried ginzo grass and wearing a big straw cowboy hat. "Can I pick 'er up?" he asked, reaching for the piece of bone.

"Sure," said Pippa, feeling her heart clench. She didn't really want anyone else to hold the bone or even to know about it. But the shop teacher was careful as he turned it over in his hand, admiring it. "I found one last summer," he said. "I was riding Serendipity—my favorite mustang at the time, real spirited mare—and I saw somethin' lying in the grass. Bright white, which you don't often see in the red dirt of the mountain. Serendipity musta seen it too 'cause she stopped right where she was. I slid off 'er, reached for it. It was a piece of scrimshaw just like yours."

"Scrimshaw," repeated Pippa, remembering the passage Kim had read about Captain Baker's house. "Is this scrimshaw?"

"Am I a buckaroo?" Bronco Bragg asked. Pippa didn't know what a buckaroo was, but she assumed that the answer was yes. It occurred to her—not for the first time—that grown-ups always went out of their way to make communication difficult. "What is scrimshaw exactly?"

"It's old," he said. "Comes from long ago, back in the terrible times when men on ships used to hunt whales. They'd sometimes keep pieces of the bones and carve pictures of things from the whaling life into them."

"So that boat, carved on mine, it's a whaling ship?"

"Has a horse got hooves?" he said with a smile.

Another question that already had an answer, she thought, but she smiled back and said, "Whaling ships and scrimshaw, those happened around the time of Captain Baker, didn't they?"

"Is rain wet?" Why doesn't he ever just say yes, Pippa wondered as he plucked the dried stick of grass from his mouth and tossed it on the shop floor. "Piece I found had a picture of a harpoon on it. Harpoon's what they used to use to kill the whales." He shuddered and took off his cowboy hat, holding it to his chest. It was a sorrowful gesture. "That was back before people knew better than to hurt wild things. Now we know we got to do what we can to help 'em."

But Pippa had stopped listening. She was thinking about Captain Baker, about the fact that he'd once had a scrimshaw collection. She wondered what had happened to it after he'd died. Had it been washed down the mountain by the wind and the weather, just like the glass windows and the wood walls in the Captain's house? If so, was it possible that the piece she'd found was from his collection? It seemed more than possible to her. It seemed likely. What else would a piece of scrimshaw be doing up on Mount Muldoon so close to the house's ruins?

Bronco Bragg was still talking. "Which is why a group of us wranglers offered to help when there was all that trouble at the Wildlife Safari Park last summer. Flooding tore the fences down. There were wild animals everywhere—zebras, elephants, giraffes. Imagine. They had to be rounded up. For their own safety. A group of us went out with our lassos. Rode around the mountain on horseback. That's when I found the scrimshaw."

"Wait," Pippa stifled a gasp. "You're saying you found your piece near the Wildlife Safari Park? On Mount Muldoon?"

"Is the moon cheese?"

Oh boy, thought Pippa. He found a piece of the Captain's collection too. So the collection must be scattered over the mountain. It must be waiting to be discovered, piece by piece. Then she registered what Bronco Bragg had said. *Is the moon cheese?* "The moon isn't cheese," she said to him. "But you do mean yes, don't you?"

"Giddyap," he said, giving a nod. Pippa smiled but inside she felt weary; it was very hard work talking to a grown-up.

"Nice job," said Bronco Bragg, gesturing to Pippa's knickknack shelf. "It's real purty."

"Thanks," Pippa said. She was already thinking about how she would use the shelf to hold all of the pieces of scrimshaw that she was going to find. She would start that night. She would find an excuse to leave the Castle and go for a walk. She wouldn't tell anyone what she was doing. She would just take a flashlight with her and keep her eyes peeled for the telltale white of a scrimshaw bone. It would be her secret.

And soon she would have a whole collection of scrimshaw to show for it.

Name four plant species that Captain Baker brought to the island on the Billy Goat. Kim felt a flush of humiliation as she remembered Mr. Petty asking her the question and how she had just stood there, not able to speak. She'd been thinking, orchids, surely, and apples, maybe. Roses? Tomatoes? Were those the answers? She hadn't even been able to get them out of her mouth when she'd taken the test in class that afternoon. Now she opened the teacher's copy of the textbook and began to scan it, looking for the answers. She noticed a damp feeling on the skin of her forearm. She lifted it and found that the sweat on her arm had made the red ink from her test bleed off the paper, leaving a big red *F* on her skin. How appropriate, she thought. Now I'm marked with the letter for failure. She knew she needed to concentrate on the words in the textbook.

Maybe dandelion is one of the plants Captain Baker brought, she wondered. Thinking this made her think about Penny and Toby playing on the grass near the playground, pulling up dandelions. If she lifted herself up in her seat and craned her neck, she could see the two of them sitting there. Oh, how she wished she was with them now, teaching Penny to crawl or tying dandelions into a lei for the baby to wear around her neck. Penny would giggle and grab the lei and pull it apart. Kim would have to take it from her before she tried to eat it. In fact, now that she thought of it, she hoped Toby knew better than to let the baby eat dandelions. Hoping to catch a glimpse of them, Kim lifted herself up in her seat and peered out the window. But the baby wasn't there anymore. Neither was Toby. Perhaps they'd gone to play on the playground. Kim ran her eyes over the climber, the slide, the seesaw, but there was no sign of Toby or the baby. Where could they have gone?

"Everything all right?" Mr. Petty looked up

from his work and frowned at Kim, who was hovering out of her chair.

Kim sat back down. "Fine," she said, even though everything wasn't fine. Kim had no idea what four plants the Captain had brought on the *Billy Goat*, she had dozens more questions to answer, and now she didn't know where Toby and the baby were.

"What's wrong with you?" asked the teacher, straightening the collar of his shirt. "Why can't you talk in public?"

"It's . . . well . . ." Kim wanted to explain that it hadn't always been this way. That she'd only just started to have this feeling of self-consciousness. "It's . . ." she tried again. "It's like . . ." When she started to talk, it was like the words were right there about to come out, but then they got stuck, and once they got stuck, they moved backwards; they slid further away. They slid deep down inside her until they were so far down that they were impossible to retrieve.

Standing in front of her teacher now, she found that she couldn't say any of this because she was experiencing it. The words were sliding further and further away. She gulped and felt a squeak come out of her wordless throat. She turned bright red and slammed her mouth shut.

"Just say it," said the teacher impatiently, but Kim shook her head. "Spit it out." Tears prickled in her eyes. Mr. Petty looked annoyed. "I may as well tell you now that tomorrow I'm going to be giving the class a public speaking assignment. You'll write a speech, memorize the speech, and then give the speech to your classmates. If you want to get a passing grade in this class, you'd better practice."

Kim felt her heart gallop with terror at the thought of giving a speech. A whole entire speech. Now all she could manage to choke out was the word, "What?"

"What topic? You're going to give a speech on why table manners are important." Kim blinked and nodded her head, although she wasn't entirely sure she knew what table manners were. The teacher must have sensed this because he grimaced and said, "Eating properly with a knife and fork, napkin in your lap, no elbows on the table . . . you know the rules. I'll give you some tips for practicing your speech." He shook his head again, then added, "You're obviously going to need them."

As soon as Mr. Petty turned back to his own work, Kim craned her neck and looked for Toby and the baby. But they were nowhere to be seen. There was nothing to do except sit back down and keep working on the test. Toby and the baby would be fine. They were probably on the track, jumping on the big foam mattress beneath the pole vault. Stop worrying about everyone else, she told herself. Concentrate on yourself. Your own problems. The test. The four plants that Captain Baker brought . . . she began to read again.

But Toby and the baby weren't at the pole vault pit. Only Kimo was there and he had no idea that he should be wondering where they were. He was caught up in a challenge of his own. After his big weekend spent carrying groceries and sailcloth up Mount Muldoon, he'd assumed that his muscles would be larger and that he would jump higher than he ever had before. But that hadn't happened. In fact, he had made two jumps so far and both of them had been fourteen feet, nine inches. That was two inches shorter than he'd jumped on Friday afternoon. Two inches. How can I be worse at jumping now than I was on Friday?

Maybe my steps were off, he thought.

It was important in pole vault to count your strides perfectly so that you could land the pole in the best spot in the pit. If your pole was too far forward, your launch would fall short; too far back, and it wouldn't happen at all. Each time before he jumped, Kimo had learned to stick the pole in the pit and to work back from there. He would mark the spot on the track where his foot needed to be in order for the pole to be placed right, and then he would count his strides backwards to a starting point at the top of the track. He knew that there were exactly seventeen strides from the top of the track to the point where he should plant his pole.

Now he stood in that spot at the top of the track and stared at the bar that was set at fifteen feet exactly. He visualized his sprint. If he took seventeen strides at the right speed, the pole would land where it should, and he would push his left hand forward on the pole, and pull his right arm back on the pole and that would launch him into the air higher than he had ever gone before.

But he had to clear his mind. Something as small as a stray leaf on the track could throw him off, and if he was at all distracted, he was likely to destroy his rhythm and ruin the jump. So it didn't help now that as he stood there, looking at the high bar, an image came into his mind: his fishing boat—the boat that he had won at the North Shore Summer Fair—dangling in the air above the ocean. He tried to wipe this image away. He tried to think about what he needed to do; he needed to sprint for seventeen steps and plant his pole in the right spot so he would soar. But this calculation only led Kimo back to the image of the boat high up in the air, dripping seawater as it hung from the crane.

Then it occurred to him that maybe he could use the image to help him concentrate. After all, wasn't he trying to break the island record so that his father would be impressed? And wasn't he keeping this a secret because he wanted to surprise his siblings when Johnny Trout suddenly changed his mind and decided not to take away their boat? The boat should be his inspiration! Picture that boat, Kimo said to himself. Use it to help you jump higher. Maybe you'll jump as high as the top of that crane.

With a renewed sense of purpose, Kimo took a deep breath, lifted his pole, and began to run. He counted his strides: one, two, three, four, five . . . when he got to seventeen, he planted his pole in the pit and jerked his arms in opposite directions so that the bending pole launched him into the air—legs first—and then he soared up and over the fifteen-foot bar. It wasn't an island record, but it wasn't too far off.

"I thought we were going to your office," Toby said as the limousine pulled into the long, curved driveway of the Royal Palm hotel.

"This *is* my office," replied Clarice, just as the driver brought the car to a stop in front of the hotel's enormous marble entrance.

A bellhop in a bright green uniform with pink coral buttons approached the car and swung open the door. "Welcome back, ma'am." He smiled at Clarice, who climbed out of the car without looking at him. But the bellhop didn't seem to mind or else he was used to this treatment. He reached into his pocket, pulled out a candy in a gold wrapper, and peered into the back of the limo. "Would sir like a mint?"

Toby blinked and looked around. Surely the bellhop wasn't talking to him. But there was no one else in the limo. I must be "sir," Toby thought, giving a little grin. "Okay," he said. "Thanks."

He could see Clarice impatiently standing under the hotel's awning, scrolling through messages on her cell phone while she waited for him. He quickly unwrapped the candy and popped it in his mouth, then he unstrapped Penny and lifted her out of the car seat. The baby reached for Toby's mouth.

"Sorry, I don't have another one," said the bellhop.

"She shouldn't have candy anyway," said Toby, impressed that the bellhop had understood the baby's gesture. Maybe he had a little sister too. Maybe he should ask the bellhop if it was odd that Penny hadn't learned to crawl yet. But the bellhop was already stepping away, holding open the door for Toby. So Toby just grabbed Goldie's jar, lifted the baby onto his hip, and stepped out of the limo.

"Leave the fish," Clarice called out. It wasn't

a suggestion, but Toby didn't care. He shot back, "He'll get hot in the car."

"We won't be long," said Clarice. "And I'll have the driver leave the AC on."

"That's bad for the environment and the planet," said Toby, reminded once again of how children were much better at taking care of things than adults.

"Then he'll park in the shade with the windows down."

Toby thought that this was reasonable, so, holding the baby, he ducked back into the limo to set down Goldie's jar. He saw that the little window between the driver and the passengers was now rolled down. "Excuse me," he said to the driver as he scooted up the long seat toward him. "I'm going to leave my fish. I hope that's okay. That Clarice lady says you're going to park in the shade so he doesn't get too hot."

Toby saw that it was the same man-in-the-moon-faced driver he had seen before and felt relieved for some reason. The man nodded and said in a low, warm baritone, "You may of course leave your aquatic friend with me." He was wearing a black hat that almost looked like a ship captain's. "I will do my utmost to keep a close watch on him and make sure his temperature doesn't elevate too much. I often leave the limousine when I'm on break, so tell me, would you object to my taking your pelagic friend with me? I would bring him to a waiting area in the basement of the hotel where I sit with other employees, the kitchen staff, the bellhops. I can assure you it's very cool down there, temperature-wise. But if you are at all uncomfortable with this arrangement, I will stay in the vehicle with your elegant friend. What would you prefer for me to do?"

By the time the driver had finished speaking, Toby's eyes were wide with surprise and his mouth had dropped open (he himself looked like the man in the moon). The only time the boy could remember having heard anyone speak in this way was when he'd gone with all the other kindergartners to listen to the fourth graders reading speeches by Abraham Lincoln. He knew he could trust "Honest Abe" with his fish, and so, he thought, he could trust this driver. "I would appreciate it if you would take him with you," Toby said, uttering perhaps the most formal sentence he had ever uttered in his life. Shifting Penny onto the other hip, he handed Goldie's jar through the open window.

"Hurry up!" Clarice shouted from beneath the hotel's awning. "Tick, tock!"

"Gotta zip," said Toby, sliding across the seats

and toward the door, then adding, "Hey, wait. What's your name?"

"My name is Coriolanus," said the driver. "But you can call me Leon."

Penny rode on Toby's hip as Clarice led them through the hotel, past the front desk and two more smiling bellhops in green uniforms who were stationed between enormous flower arrangements. "Welcome back, ma'am," they both said as Clarice walked by them and pushed the button beside the elevator. While they waited, Toby stared at his reflection in the shiny gold doors and bounced Penny in his arms. He was trying to remember if the baby had ever ridden in an elevator. He thought that she probably hadn't, so when the doors slid open, he said, "This is an elevator—"

"I know that," Clarice said.

"I'm talking to Penny," said Toby, stepping through the doors. "She's never been in one before."

"So?"

"So I'm telling her about it, so she won't be scared." For someone who ran a company that sold baby products, Clarice seemed to know very little about how to take care of a baby.

"Huh," said Clarice, touching a plastic fob to the keypad so that she could press the button for the twelfth floor. The doors shut and the elevator began to rise.

"It's like a little room that takes you up and down. It's easier than stairs." Toby nuzzled the baby. "And it's easier than climbing Mount Muldoon at the end of every day."

"Why would you say that?" Clarice asked.

"'Cause that's where we're living," Toby bragged. "We found Captain Baker's old castle up there and we took it over." As soon as the words were out of his mouth, he regretted them. What if Clarice got it into her head to come and take the Castle from them? "It's not actually a castle," he quickly corrected. "It's just a lot of rocks shaped like a house." Clarice shrugged, took out her cell phone and began typing into it. So maybe she wasn't even listening, Toby thought. The elevator stopped and the doors slid open. "See," Toby said to the baby. "Just like magic—we're on the twelfth floor."

"Wimo," said Penny.

"Yeah," said Toby, who could see the baby's point. "It is a lot like a limo. It's fancy and it takes you places." The baby grabbed hold of Toby's hair as they stepped into a large, high-ceilinged room with more enormous flower arrangements. There were several plush sofas and in the center of each seating area was a wide, low coffee-table where magazines were fanned out like the tails of peacocks. There was a small kitchen with a gleaming silver fridge, cabinets, a sink, and a countertop with a coffee maker and an electric teakettle. It didn't look to Toby like a place where work got done. It looked like a place where rich people made coffee, then sat and drank it and talked about whatever rich people talked about. Money, proba-bly. He turned to Clarice. "Where do you work?"

"This is the foyer," said Clarice. "My offices are that way." She gestured to the left. "My apart-ment is that way." She gestured to the right.

"So you live here?"

"Do you always ask so many questions?"

Toby felt like telling her that she had just asked a question, but then he realized that that was no way to win a contest. In fact, it was pos-sible that the contest had already started and that he was being judged right now. If so, he could tell from the weary expression on Clarice's face that he wasn't doing very well. So it was a relief when Clarice said, "The contest will start as soon as Benicio gets here. In the meantime, how about some room service?"

"Sure," said Toby hesitantly. He didn't under-stand exactly what service she wanted him to perform. "Do I sweep? Or vacuum? Or what?"

This made Clarice laugh. "Room service is

something you get, not something you give," she said, then she pointed to an old-fashioned telephone sitting on one of the coffee-tables. "Try it." Confused, Toby tugged on his ear. "Go ahead," she said.

Still holding the baby, Toby reached for the telephone. He put his ear to the receiver the way he'd seen Kim and Kimo do when they had made telephone calls.

A chirpy voice came from the other end of the line. "Room service," it said.

"Hi," said Toby. "Okay." He still had no idea what was going on.

"Do you know what you'd like?"

"Um," said Toby. "I'd like room service."

"Okay," said the voice. "Open the menu." Toby spotted the menu lying beside the phone. He did as instructed. "Now whattaya want?" the voice asked.

Now Toby understood that room service was a way to order food. And what a menu! There were so many things that Toby loved: hamburgers, hot dogs, French fries, ice cream sundaes. What to get? He looked up at Clarice.

"Whatever you want," she said, anticipating his question.

"I'll have one of everything." He looked down at the baby. "Oh, and I'd better order something for my sister too."

"Don't," said Clarice. "We've got all kinds of baby food right here." She opened one of the cabinets in the little kitchen, revealing dozens of jars of Baby Loves baby food. Of course there was food for Penny; this was the office of Baby Loves. (Toby saw that the magazines on the coffee-tables were all copies of *Baby Loves Magazine*.)

"Never mind," Toby said to the voice on the other end of the phone. "Nothing for my sister. Just for me."

"Okay," said the voice. "Coming right up!"

A few minutes later, the elevator doors opened, and another bellhop pushed a large cart into the room and straight toward Toby. On it were many

plates covered with
metal lids and a
small bucket of ice
with an ice cream
sundae poking out
of it. The cart of food
was possibly the
most exciting meal
Toby had ever seen,

so it was amazing that he immediately looked away from it and toward the man
stepping off the elevator behind it.

The man was wearing a marvelous outfit that
featured all the colors of the rainbow: a shirt of
red, pink, blue, and green and a pair of orange-
and-yellow pants. On the man's feet were sneakers
covered in dazzling silver glitter. Toby had never
worn shoes in his life, but looking at those sneakers he decided that if he ever did, he would wear
a pair just like that. In fact, Toby wanted to have
an outfit exactly like the man's, including the silver

umbrella that the man was pulling out from under his arm and opening.

"Is it going to rain?" Toby asked, and the man began to laugh, a laugh that sounded like coins dropping to the ground.

"Funny," he said.

"This is Benicio. He's a photographer," Clarice explained just as Benicio pulled a huge camera out of one of the bags that hung from around his neck.

"I hope you brought a backdrop," Clarice said to him.

"I brought three," Benicio said, and he pulled a long tube out of one of the bags and began to unroll the backdrops, which were large photographs of outdoor settings: a grassy field, a riverbank, a mountaintop.

"I don't think we want a picture of a baby on a mountaintop," Clarice said. "Let's go with the grass. We'll make it look like a picnic."

Just then the smell of French fries filled the room. Toby turned and saw that the bellhop had lifted the metal lids off the plates. Steam was rising from the fries, which looked perfect: crisp and greasy at the same time.

"Why don't you eat," suggested Clarice. "And we'll start the contest."

"Is it an eating contest?" asked Toby. He was thinking about *Ham!*, the show where contestants ate sausages while telling jokes.

"I told you he was funny," said Benicio.

But Clarice wasn't amused. "It's a photo contest," she said to Toby. "We take pictures of all the contestants and then we decide whose picture is best. So you go ahead and eat while your food is hot."

Toby wanted to eat those fries more than he'd ever wanted to eat anything. But what if this was a test? What if it was part of the contest to see if he chose to get his picture taken or to eat the food? He decided he didn't care. As far as he was concerned, he had already won. Those French fries were the best prize anyone could ask for. "Okay," he said.

"Good," said Clarice. "We'll get started taking her photograph." She pointed at the baby.

Toby lifted the baby up over his head and wiggled his tongue at her. "You want to get your picture taken?"

"My do it," the baby pronounced.

"Great," said Toby, adding, "Don't worry, I'll be right here." He set the baby down on the carpet, then he crossed the room and sat himself down in front of the cart of fantastic food.

CHAPTER

9

That night, as they sat around the kitchen fireplace eating bowls of chili, Toby forced himself to take a few small bites. He didn't want to draw attention to the fact that he wasn't hungry, but the truth was that his stomach was swollen with all of the magnificent food that he had eaten at the Royal Palm hotel.

After the French fries, there had been a hamburger, a hot dog, a grilled cheese sandwich, a steak, a plate of fish and chips, and something called a French dip, which was a meat sandwich that came with a little bowl of soup. He'd eaten steadily while Clarice had spooned Baby Loves baby food into Penny's mouth, and Benicio had called out to the baby, "Smile," as he took her photograph. Benicio's silver umbrella flashed every time he clicked his camera, and the baby—giggling and beaming—was delighted by the effect. "Smile," Benicio said, "Smile!" Penny seemed—to Toby—to genuinely enjoy all the attention.

Toby's meal had taken so long for him to eat that by the time he'd finished the ice cream sundae, there was no time for him to get *his* photograph taken by Benicio. "We have to get back before anyone notices," he told Clarice, and she shrugged and said, "Fine." It occurred to Toby then that perhaps the CEO of Baby Loves didn't care about taking his picture; perhaps all along she'd only ever planned to take pictures of Penny eating baby food. But he decided that was okay with him. No harm had been done. He'd had a tremendous meal and a very good time; Penny had too. They had left the penthouse and Leon, the driver, had returned Goldie, who seemed to have enjoyed his cool afternoon in the hotel's staff area. Leon had driven Toby and Penny back to the same spot in the grass at Windward School just in time for Kim and the others to pick them up. Toby could tell because all the dandelions in that area were pulled up or crushed.

Now Toby was poking at his bowl of chili, trying to force himself to take another bite, and Pippa was on her feet, holding her empty bowl and offering to wash all the dishes by herself. At another time, Toby might have considered this offer strangely generous, but he was too busy hiding his own odd behavior to notice Pippa's.

"Thanks," said Kim, handing Pippa her empty bowl. "I have to start my homework."

When Pippa reached for Toby's bowl, she saw that it was still mostly full. "You didn't eat anything."

"Yes, I did," said Toby.

Kim thought about the online article she had printed out before coming home from school: "A Brief History of Table Manners." "Finishing everything you are served is one of the most important table manners," Kim said to Toby.

"We don't have a table," said Pippa.

"It doesn't matter," replied Kim, who had thought about the same thing. "Table manners are important for any eating occasion, even a picnic."

Toby remembered the picnic photos of Penny. He didn't want to tell an outright lie, but he didn't want to tell the whole truth either. "I might have a stomachache," he said.

Penny was not so guarded. "Wimo," she said.

"You *might* have a stomachache?" Kim was focused on Toby and not the baby.

"I do have a stomachache."

"Mile," the baby said.

Kimo looked at the baby. "She's trying to tell us something," he said.

"No, she's not," said Toby.

"Mile," Penny said again. This time, as if for emphasis, she grabbed hold of her foot and stretched out her leg.

"She's talking nonsense," said Toby, who knew full well that the baby was repeating Benicio's word, "smile."

"She usually means something," Kimo pointed out. "She doesn't talk for no reason."

"Sure she does," said Toby. "You should have heard her this afternoon. Talk, talk, talk . . ." He trailed off, regretting having brought up his time with the baby that afternoon. He didn't want anyone to ask him for specifics. He decided to change tactics and said, "Anyway, whatever she's trying to say, she seems happy about it." And this observation was enough to allow the older siblings to shift their focus away from the baby and onto their own pressing concerns.

Pippa was filling the cooler with dirty dishes, already thinking about how after she washed them she would search the area farther downstream from the waterfall for more of Captain Baker's scrimshaw. Kim was opening her backpack and getting out her textbooks. She was worried about how she'd get all her homework done before dark.

"You want help?" Kimo asked.

"No," said Pippa. "I got it."

Kimo looked happy to be absolved of doing dishes and immediately began to climb one of the branches that reached into the house. "I'm going to do chin-ups," he said. "I wish we had a real chin-up bar." It was hard to practice while hanging from a tree branch, because the branches that were thin enough to hold swayed and bent as he did the exercises. Maybe he wouldn't do them after all; maybe he would just close his eyes and spend some time imagining his pole-vaulting sprint. Ms. Bonicle had told him that most record breakers used visualization to improve their performance.

Toby sat holding his mostly full bowl of chili and watching the others head off. He couldn't remember the last time they'd spent an evening completely apart. Something strange is happening, he thought, but he wasn't the kind of boy to spend time wondering what it was.

Pippa *was* the sort to wonder about strange things, and as she sat with her feet in the pool at the base of the waterfall, scrubbing the dishes with mud and grit, she pondered the change that was happening within her little family. It occurred to her that for the first time ever, she and her siblings had a place to call their own, a place that was really theirs, a place they didn't have to worry about losing. No one was going to say the Castle wasn't theirs (like Johnny Trout's cabin) and no one was going to take it away with a crane (like the boat) and they weren't going to outgrow it like the car. That they were free from these worries gave them the opportunity to think about other things, things like finding scrimshaw.

She found herself shouting, "Yeehaw! Yee-haw! Yeehaw!" as if she were some miniature, bespectacled version of Bronco Bragg. Then she clapped her hand over her mouth, suddenly fearful that her siblings would hear her and ask her what she was shouting about and why the heck she sounded like a rodeo star. It would be hard to explain how Bronco Bragg had inspired her without explaining about the piece of scrimshaw—and that wasn't a secret she was willing to give away yet. Then she realized that her fear of being heard was absurd. Any noise she had made had surely been drowned out by the loud roar of the waterfall. "Yeehaw," she shouted again, giving the last couple of plates a vigorous scrub.

When the dishes were done, she set them in the cooler and got to her feet. She would leave the cooler where it was while she went off on her scrimshaw hunt. "Yeehaw," she whooped one last time for good measure. Her piece of scrimshaw sat on a nearby rock beside her flashlight. "What a beaut," she said, turning the bone over in her hands and then sliding it into her pocket. She grabbed the flashlight; even though the moon was full and bright, she would need it for the hunt.

But how to begin? She wished that she had a map of the mountain so that she could cross off the areas that she'd searched once she'd searched them. It would help her to keep track. I'll just have to keep a map in my mind, she thought. It'll be a challenge. She decided she would walk the edge of the stream that flowed from the waterfall. It made sense to her that if she'd found one piece of scrimshaw near the water, there might be others that had been washed farther downstream.

She clicked on the flashlight and carefully began to pick her way along the pebbled shore. As she walked, she waved the flashlight's beam back and forth across her path. She was scanning for any sign of whiteness that might signal another piece of bone. Almost immediately, she saw something that looked promising, but when she bent to pick it up, she discovered it was a milk-colored blossom from a booligah bush. Then, with an inward groan, she realized there were booligah blossoms everywhere. In fact, booligah bushes lined the shore of the stream for as far as she could see.

Should I walk farther from the stream? she wondered, and then answered herself in the manner of Bronco Bragg: Is a booligah blossom white? So she headed into the canopy of trees. She didn't need to find any particular path because the pebbles and rocks gave way to hard-packed soil stretching in an arc around her. It was a promising area to search because the ground was so clear; very little was growing, since the tall canopy of trees let in very little sunlight. Walking slowly, she fanned the flashlight in an arc in front of her, and her eyes followed it, searching in every direction.

As she moved farther from the waterfall, she began to be able to hear the noises of the forest—the sound of branches moving as the birds settled into their nests for the night, the whirr of insect wings . . . those must be pretty big insects if I can hear their wings, she thought. It was a thought that made her stop walking for a moment because it led her to another, even more disturbing thought: what about the slurp and the rustle they had heard the other night? What if whatever monsters had made those sounds happened to be taking an after-dinner stroll through this part of the forest? Even worse, what if those monsters hadn't yet had dinner? What if they decided that a brown-haired, brown-eyed, freckled girl was the perfect appetizer—or even main course?

Pippa instinctively lowered herself closer to the ground. She knew that she should probably shout the way she had shouted the other night; that would scare the monsters away. But since she hadn't yet heard the rustle or the slurp, it seemed to make more sense not to draw attention to herself. She would just stay small and keep quiet. She would listen and she would keep the flashlight turned on so she could shine the light into the eyes of any monsters that approached. This would blind them for long enough that she could run away. To that end, she began to trace the flashlight's beam over the ground around her. And that is when she saw something that made a shiver of terror run down her spine.

A few feet in front of her was a very large footprint. Only that was the wrong word. It wasn't a print made by a foot; it was a print made by something else. Something stranger. It might have been a paw print or a hoof print except it was about three times as large as either of those. She crouched low to the ground and quickly shuffled toward it. Shining the flashlight directly on it, she traced its outline with her fingers. Now she could tell that it was composed of two moon-shaped halves that faced each other. Where had she seen that shape

before? She remembered the Halloween costume parade at school when Kainoa P. had dressed as the Grim Reaper.

The Grim Reaper carried a scythe just like the two shapes pressed into the ground.

Pippa's heart began to thud in her chest, a noise so loud that she was sure whatever had made the prints would be able to hear it. Take a deep breath, she thought. Be calm. Be logical. Just because you think of the Grim Reaper when you look at these prints doesn't mean they were made by the Grim Reaper. Besides, Kainoa P.'s scythe was plastic. It was about as dangerous as a rubber chicken. Maybe this thing isn't dangerous either.

She moved the flashlight even closer and adjusted her glasses, squinting at the print again. She decided that it was about the size of a football. A print that size belonged to something way too big not to be dangerous.

She stepped back and turned slowly in a circle, beaming the flashlight around her. Now she saw that there wasn't just one print. There was a line of prints leading out of the dark forest across the packed dirt and toward the stream—which meant that the monster was walking in the direction of the Castle. She felt a clammy sweat break out on her hands and feet. *Bang, bang, bang*—her heart was pounding like a hammer against a concrete wall.

Should I run and tell the others?

In her mind, she heard Bronco Bragg drawling,

Is there a monster with scythe-shaped prints the size of footballs moving in their direction?

The answer was yes.

With a jerk, she shot into motion and crossed the packed dirt clearing in a matter of seconds. Her arms churning at her sides, she turned and almost immediately found herself facing a steep hill covered in low bushes. Waving the flashlight frantically in front of her, she began making her way up, dodging and leaping over the shrubs, gulping air so she could go faster. She was making quick progress up the treacherous incline. There's nothing quite like the picture of a hungry, scythe-footed monster making a meal out of your siblings to get you moving, Pippa was thinking even as her left foot caught in a tangle of branches and she stumbled. The hill was so steep she didn't have far to go before she smacked down on the ground and her glasses got knocked off as she did a face-plant between the bushes. She'd had one hand on the flashlight and one hand holding closed the pocket that held her piece of scrimshaw, so she'd been unable to get her hands out in front of her to block her own fall.

Lying in the dirt, she made a mental checklist of all her body parts. She could feel some scratches on her face and there was the taste of blood in her mouth, so she must have bitten her tongue. She felt around on the ground beside her for her glasses and slid them back on, then she blinked to see if her vision was blurry (it wasn't) and scrambled to her knees. And that was when she noticed moonlight glinting off something that was half-buried in the ground beside her. Just another booligah blossom, she thought, but she trained the flashlight on it to be sure. In the bright beam she could see that it was nothing like a flower; it was hard and smooth and had the appearance of a large tooth.

She began to dig away the dirt that surrounded it, unearthing it in a matter of seconds. She pulled it out and studied it in the flashlight beam. It was a small bone—yes, most definitely a bone—but was it scrimshaw? The white part that had been sticking out of the ground had no carvings on it, and the end that had been buried was too covered in dirt and mud for her to know. She worked up a big ball of spit in her mouth and plopped it onto the bone, then she rubbed at the bone with her T-shirt. Now she could see just what she'd been hoping for—a carved picture of a whale thrashing in the ocean. So it was a piece of scrimshaw. She felt her heart hammering again, only this time it was with excitement.

She studied the intricate carving which showed a whale with a huge square head. The whale's large upper jaw and a thin lower jaw were open enough to reveal terrifying white teeth. Its body was hidden beneath the thin, carved lines that suggested water, but the animal's wide powerful tail rose up out of the water and looked like it was about to splash down right on top of a rowboat filled with terrified sailors.

Pippa ran her finger over the carving of the sailors. She could feel the tiny little scratches that formed their faces and it occurred to her how impressive it was that the artist had been able to make her feel the sailor's terror with such a few thin strokes. The sailors looked as frightened as she had felt only a few moments ago. Now she didn't feel frightened. What she felt was thrilled; she had found a second piece of scrimshaw even more impressive and detailed than the first.

She pulled the first piece out of her pocket and looked at the two of them side by side. They almost told a story. She could imagine the sailors on the three-masted ship that was shown on the first piece of scrimshaw launching a small rowboat and going out to hunt the whale that was on the second piece. The whale must have been furious at their attack. And didn't he fight back with his terrifying teeth, his powerful spout, and his massive, muscular tail?

It was this thought—of an angry creature lashing out—that made Pippa remember herself. She was supposed to be running back to the Castle to save her brothers and sisters from the hungry, rustling scythe-monster. But she didn't want to. She felt no urge to run. Why not?

She began to reason through the impulse she'd had when she'd first seen those scythe prints. I don't even know if those prints are recent or if they were made days or even weeks ago, she thought. There's nothing about them to suggest that they're fresh. In fact, if she really considered it, they'd looked a little blurred or washed out—like they had been there for a while. Now she couldn't remember why she'd ever thought that the rustling monster was on its way to the Castle *now*. And even if it was, why did she think it would hurt any of them? What if it was like the whale on the piece of scrimshaw? What if it only lashed out when it was being attacked? After all, the rustling monster hadn't hurt them when they'd heard it near the Castle a few nights before. It had run away when they'd made noise. Really, Pippa thought, there's no need to run and there's no need to tell anyone what I've seen. They'll just get worried, and isn't it nice for all of us that for once we're living somewhere without any worries? That was exactly what Pippa had been telling herself earlier in the evening while she scrubbed dishes by the waterfall.

Of course, she would never let her brothers and sisters be hurt. She would keep on the lookout for the rustling monster, and she would make sure the alarms were in place, but she would not trouble anyone else by telling them about the scythe prints. There was no reason to make them unnecessarily upset.

Even as Pippa was deciding not to run back to the Castle or tell anyone about the prints, she wondered about her own motives. Deep, deep,

deep down—as deep down in the ocean as a whale goes when it is hiding from attacking sailors—Pippa feared that if she told her siblings about the prints they would decide it was best to leave the Castle for good. And that meant that she would not be able to continue her hunt for scrimshaw—which was absolutely unacceptable. Having one piece of scrimshaw had made Pippa want two. But having two pieces made her want not just three pieces but four pieces or five or a dozen. In fact, if she told herself the truth, she wanted all the pieces she could have; she wanted Captain Baker's entire scrimshaw collection! So she would not give up the Castle. And why should she?

While Pippa was debating whether a monster was headed toward the Castle, Kim was sitting on the ground beside the fireplace doing her homework. She had her textbook and her notebook propped up on a log and she was working on her last math problem: *Jane puts an amoeba in a jar at 1:00. The*

amoeba quadruples in number every twenty min-
utes. How many amoebas will be in the jar at 5:00?
She had drawn a column of different times—1:00,
1:20, 1:40, 2:00, all the way to 5:00—and had begun
to draw pictures of all the amoebas for each of those
times. But the more she worked, and the more
amoebas she drew, the more Kim realized she was
leaning closer and closer to the paper to see them
clearly. The Castle was very dark at night; moonlight barely penetrated the canopy of branches.
She hadn't even begun to write her speech on table
manners and already it was getting dark.

She got up and fished around in her backpack for the flashlight, then remembered that Pippa had taken it when she went to do the dishes. Where was Pippa? What was taking her so long? Was it possible that Pippa had met with Captain Baker's ghost? Kim banished this thought, reminding herself that she needed to stay focused on her work.

That afternoon she'd written a new to-do list in the margins of her notebook and, for the first time ever, it wasn't filled with things that her family needed her to do. It was filled with things that she needed to do for herself:

Math problem set 7
Write speech on table manners
Read history chapters 7 and 8
Science fair brainstorm

But how would she complete her list if she couldn't see her homework? She burrowed deeper into the backpack until she found a candle and a box of matches. She moved back to the fireplace and lit the candle. Using the flame from a couple of matches, she melted the bottom of the candle and let the wax drip into a puddle on the fireplace stones, then she pushed the candle into the melted wax. Once it had cooled down, and the wax had hardened, the candle was sealed into place so that it stood upright.

The light wasn't very good, but if she leaned in close, she could just barely see her pencil on the paper. She finished the last math problem quickly, arriving at a dizzying number of amoebas, and put it away. Then she got out the article that she had printed before leaving school, and she began to read. "It's important to treat the table—and every meal you eat at it—with respect. When you sit in your chair, avoid slouching. Put your napkin in your lap."

Just then, Pippa appeared, carrying the cooler of clean dishes, and apologizing. "Sorry it took me so long."

It occurred to Kim that most of the students who would be writing speeches on table manners did not do their dishes in a waterfall. "What happened?" she asked. "About a million amoebas could've been born while you were gone."

Pippa set down the cooler. "Am I supposed to know what that means?"

"I was just starting to wonder if you were okay."

"There's nothing to be afraid of, if that's what you mean," said Pippa. Then, trying to change the subject, she gestured to the article. "What're you reading?"

Kim ignored her. "Are you sure you were okay doing dishes alone? I mean, now that I think about it, with that weird noise the other night, we probably should be going to the waterfall in pairs."

"Don't be ridiculous." Pippa gave a sinister laugh to make clear just how un-scared she'd been.

"Laugh like that and you'll scare anything away."

"Exactly," said Pippa, heading off to the

corner of the mansion where her hammock hung. "'Night."

"'Night," said Kim, watching her little sister disappear into the darkness. If she'd been paying attention, Kim might have noticed that Pippa's pockets were bulging, but she was busy with her own thoughts. Under the spell of the Castle, the children were forgetting to look after each other. It hadn't hurt anyone yet, but the Family Monster Calamity would soon be upon them.

CHAPTER
10

In the days that followed, the Fitzgerald-Trout children were drawn further and further into their own private pursuits. After school, Kimo would stay at the track to practice pole vaulting and Kim would drive Pippa, Toby, and Penny back to Mount Muldoon. Once they were home, Pippa would head off, saying that she wanted to pick guavas or go for a swim, and Kim would check her to-do list, which now consisted only of her own homework. Top of the list was practicing her speech on table manners. She had been given practice techniques by Mr. Petty, one of which was to bite down on a pencil as she loudly enunciated the words she had written and memorized. "Good manners at the table are important . . ." With the pencil between her teeth, this sounded like "Goot mayonnaise adda tabe ill arr imprudent." As she practiced, she paced the Castle. If she noticed the piles of dirty clothes that meant it was time to do laundry, she ignored them. The problem was that everyone else ignored them too.

Toby spent his afternoons in his "room" with Penny, who had chosen him as her favorite babysitter. He knew Penny preferred him because she now associated him with the ride in the limousine and up in the elevator and the entertaining afternoon she'd spent in the office of Baby Loves eating as much baby food as she wanted, but he didn't tell this to the others. He was glad to be the favorite older sibling of the moment and enjoyed entertaining Penny by swinging from the vines in his room or playing the bongo drums that Mr. Knuckles had given him. Sometimes he tried to teach the baby to crawl, demonstrating how to move forward on his feet and hands, then sitting back and waiting for the baby to imitate him. "Crawl," he would say. "Come on, Penny, crawl." But the baby never did.

After a while he would stop these lessons and just lie back in the moss and daydream. He watched the breeze ruffle the sailcloth roof and the bees buzzing in the orchids that grew from the stone walls of the Castle. He told Penny stories about Tobyworld, a kingdom ruled by a boy and his pet goldfish. There were no cities or streets in Tobyworld, there were only forests and beaches. "In Tobyworld," he told the baby, "I can swim with Goldie, only swimming is like flying because you can breathe under water." If the baby was confused by these stories, she didn't let on. She smiled and drooled and sometimes shouted,

"Up!"—which meant she wanted Toby to lie on his back and use his feet to fly her in the air. So maybe she did understand.

While Penny was flying, and Toby was daydreaming, and Pippa was treasure hunting, and Kim was pacing and pronouncing with the pencil between her teeth, Kimo was back at the school track, practicing his vaulting. His PE teacher, and now track coach, Ms. Bonicle, was convinced her star athlete would soon be breaking the island record. There was a meet coming up, and Ms. Bonicle hoped to draw a crowd big enough to inspire Kimo to soar up and up and up and over that fifteen-foot-and-two-inch mark.

She had put an announcement in the school newspaper:

COME SEE WINDWARD SCHOOL'S
VERY OWN KIMO FITZGERALD-TROUT
AS HE ATTEMPTS TO BREAK THE
ISLAND RECORD FOR POLE VAULTING

WHERE: WINDWARD SCHOOL

WHEN: SATURDAY, JANUARY 23

DURING THE TRACK MEET.

RAIN OR SHINE.

Ms. Bonicle had photocopied the announcement and hung the flyers all over the school, and even in places in town—the library, the city hall, the post office—so that all day long, no matter where he was, any time Kimo turned a corner, he saw another one. After a day spent reading those flyers, Kimo arrived at the track inspired, thrilled to work hard.

Mrs. Bonicle had him running two miles and then doing dozens and dozens of sprints and many pull-ups, push-ups, and sit-ups before he even picked up the pole. After that "warm-up," there was the actual pole vaulting—or, as Mrs. Bonicle put it, *"Swish, swish, pop, zow-wee!"* These were the sounds she told Kimo that he should hear in his head as he was doing each vault. The *swish* was the sound of his legs sprinting down the track taking his seventeen strides, the *pop* was the moment he planted the pole on the ground, and the *zow-wee* was the sound he was supposed to hear when he flipped upside down and twisted himself over the bar. *Swish, swish, pop, zow-wee! Swish, swish, pop, zow-wee! Swish, swish, pop, zow-wee!* Just when he thought if he heard those sounds in his head one more time, his muscles would give up entirely, Ms. Bonicle would tell him it was time to stop. But practice wasn't over, oh no. Now it was time to lift weights. Kim had once called Kimo "Mega Muscles," and it was fitting: he lifted the weights Ms. Bonicle demanded with the ferocious intensity of a circus strongman.

Practice, practice, practice, he said to himself as he lifted. He thought those words were the punchline to an old joke, but he didn't know what the joke was. He only knew that if the entire school came to the track meet and he knocked the bar off instead of clearing it, the joke would be on him.

After Ms. Bonicle released him from his training session, Kimo would have to get home on his own. He used the mile-and-a-half jog to the foot of Mount Muldoon as a "warm-down" from his workout. He loved the time alone and the feeling of having worked hard. He didn't know what to call the last part of the journey when he climbed up the mountain to the Castle. He was beyond warming down at that point; he was just exhausted, and he usually arrived just as the sun was setting and his siblings were starting to make dinner. Of course, he helped with that too.

His practice was so hard that one night, by the time they were eating, he barely had the energy necessary to chase his peas from his plate onto his spoon. All he could hear in his head was *swish, swish, pop, zow-wee!* He sat eating in utter silence. Kim was quiet that night too. She had a vocabulary quiz the following day and was flipping through flashcards while she ate, saying each of the vocabulary words under her breath, then testing herself on the spelling: "Millennium. *M-I-L-L-E-N-N-I-U-M.*"

Pippa was plopped on the ground near the fireplace, thinking through her mental map of the mountain. She was picturing the spot around the waterfall where she'd first searched and the wide area of hard-packed dirt where she'd found the prints. She'd been back there several times in daylight to look for more scrimshaw, and she knew just how much ground she'd covered. "I should walk down from there to the other side of Gasper's Gulch," she was saying to herself, when suddenly a pea hit her right in the eye. "Hey." She looked up at Toby, who she knew was responsible. He had his wrist cocked and was launching peas at Kimo and Kim too.

"Throwing food is bad table manners," Kim said.

"Say you're sorry." Pippa fired one of her peas at him.

Toby ducked the pea. "I'm not gonna say I'm sorry. Something's wrong with you guys."

"Nothing's wrong with us," said Pippa. "Something's wrong with YOU."

"Nuh-uh," said Toby. "Penny thinks so too."

He looked down at the baby, who shouted, "My do it," then grabbed her foot and put it in her mouth.

"The way you're acting," Toby continued. "Whispering to yourselves, and . . . what's that word? Muttering. Yeah, muttering. You'd think some kind of weird bug bit you and turned you all into zombies."

"Do zombies mutter?" asked Pippa. "Because in the zombie literature I've read, that is *not* one of their characteristics."

"They act crazy," said Toby. "And you guys are acting crazy, like you've been . . . you know," he was searching for the word, and then he found it, "possessed."

"If you had the homework I have," said Kim, feeling a strange pride at the thought of all her hard work, "you'd feel possessed."

"If you had the workouts I have," said Kimo, feeling a similar contented pride, "well, you would be possessed. There wouldn't be anything in your brain except *swish, swish, pop, zow-wee!*"

"I have no idea what that means," said Pippa, who wasn't about to confess to being possessed by treasure hunting.

"We're just happy being busy," said Kim.

"Busy being happy," said Kimo.

"Both," said Pippa.

"And I'm just reminding you," said Toby, "we used to joke around and now . . . it's like . . . we're all . . ." He trailed off, shrugging and tossing the rest of his peas into his mouth. He got to his feet and lifted the baby onto his hip. "Forget it," he said, starting toward his corner of the Castle.

"Boy," said Pippa. "What's wrong with him?"

Kim shrugged and ignored Toby's outburst. "I've got to practice my speech. Pippa, will you do the dishes?" She had come to rely on Pippa to volunteer for this duty.

"Sure," said Pippa. "I could use the walk." Pippa got up and began to collect the dirty dishes. She was already thinking about just how far she would search that night. She hadn't found another piece of scrimshaw since the piece with the whale on it, but her enthusiasm for hunting was unabated.

"I'm going to do homework," said Kimo, shuffling toward his corner of the Castle. He had some math to do but was looking forward to dreams of pole vaulting. Halfway across the space, he thought of something and turned back. "Tobes isn't wrong, you know? We haven't done much together, not since we found this place."

Kim scowled but couldn't disagree. "How about we plan something for this weekend?"

From his corner of the Castle, in his room full of piles of dirty laundry, Toby had heard everything. "How 'bout we go to the laundromat?" he asked.

That Sunday, the Fitzgerald-Trouts piled into the car and headed out of the Muldoon Park Parking Lot in the direction of Mr. Knuckles's laundromat. The plan was to do all the laundry while they watched TV with Mr. Knuckles and ate the free chocolate bars that came out of his broken vending machine. (If they were lucky, Asha might be there with some day-old doughnuts too.)

As they turned onto the road that ran around the island, they all experienced the happy lift that comes from that first glimpse of the ocean. Seagulls rode the air beside them. Kim pressed the gas and the car struggled forward, gasping and rattling in an unhappy way that made Kimo crank the volume on the radio.

On their left was the open ocean; on their right, a sugarcane field. Everywhere else was a big sky so blue that it was startling. The first song they heard on the radio was a new hit by Toby's favorite band, The Incomplete Omelets. The song's lyrics were both catchy and confusing (the Fitzgerald-Trouts' favorite combination): "You don't have to act like you don't need me, you don't have to sing like you don't need me, you don't have to dance like you don't need me, but I love it when you do."

Pippa, who thought she knew something about romance, shook her head, mystified. "If they're in love, why does he *like* it when she doesn't need him? I mean, Mr. Knuckles doesn't want Asha to dance or sing or act like she doesn't need him."

"Maybe he does," said Kimo. "Maybe he wants her to be free and happy." He had his arm out the window and was letting his hand ride up and down on the currents of wind as the little car did its best on the hilly road.

"That's not how love works," said Pippa.

"Maybe when he says, 'but I love it when you do,' he means, 'I love it when you do need me.'"

"Quiet," hissed Toby, who was tapping on the seat in front of him like it was a drum.

"What makes you think it's a song about romance?" asked Kim. She was looking at the baby in the rearview mirror, noticing how contented Penny looked. "Maybe it's about a dad who's looking at his kid and thinking how great it is that the kid can do things on her own."

"No way," said Pippa. "It's a love song."

"Shhh," said Toby. "Stop ruining it." The chorus came on and they all chimed in, including the baby, whose version was nothing but the words, "You doe, you doe, you doe," over and over. Sitting in the front seats, Kim and Kimo glanced at each other and smiled. When they turned their eyes back to the road, they saw the strangest sight. The car was headed down a little hill, and at the bottom where the road narrowed and the beach nearly touched the edge of the sugarcane field there was—on the beach side—a giant pool of something brown and sludgy. But what?

"Chocolate," said Kim.

"Chocolate," said Kimo.

"Chocolate," said Pippa.

"Poop," said Toby.

"Chocolate or poop?" asked Kim. "Let's go see." At the bottom of the hill, she pulled over to the shoulder of the road and brought the car to a stop. They all clambered out. Looking both ways, they crossed the street, then scrambled down a small incline and found themselves at the edge of the dark, thick lake. If it was chocolate, it was a dream come true. If it was poop . . . well, yuck.

"Only one way to find out," said Toby. "Smell it."

"You smell it," Pippa countered.

"I'm holding the baby," said Kim, bowing out.

So it was good-natured Kimo who knelt down and drew in a deep breath, motioning the scent toward his nostrils with a wave of his hand. He didn't say anything. Instead, he picked up a stick and, like a scientist studying an alien life-form, he poked at the mysterious substance. Then he must have thought it wasn't poop because he scooped up a little bit in his right hand and rubbed it between his fingers. When he was satisfied with his conclusion, he stood up, looked at the others, and solemnly pronounced, "Mud." All at once, the Fitzgerald-Trouts let out a whoop of joy. Mud! What could be better than a pond of mud?

Pippa took the plunge first, barreling into the murky stuff and screaming, "I'm the Creature from the Black Lagoon." Toby ran toward her and then executed a pirouette, falling backwards into the deep pudding. Kimo just belly-flopped down, holding his hands in front of his face so he wouldn't get any in his eyes, and Kim, who was still carrying Penny, waded out and dug a hand into it, squeezing a big gob between her fingers. Soon they were all up to their necks. They passed the baby around, watching her giggling with glee as her toes and feet and then legs and knees were dipped in, like a dyed Easter egg.

Have you ever been in a bubble bath? That's what this was like, a giant bubble bath, only instead of soft, clean white bubbles, the Fitzgerald-Trouts frolicked in smooth, brown, squoozable, squinchable mud. They dipped their heads back into it and covered their hair and then molded their locks into strange and inspired styles. They smeared it on their faces like warriors and then they mud wrestled. They lay backward and moved their arms and legs in wide arcs, making mud angels. Like a comedian from an old black-and-white movie, Toby kept pretending to slip and fall face-first into it. Once, when he lifted himself out, Pippa looked at him—he was absolutely slathered in dark mud— and she said, as if they were in some kind of fancy restaurant and he had a crumb on his lip, "Uh,

Tobes, you've got a little something on your face."
This made everyone crack up.

As fun as all of this mud bathing was, the greatest part came when they climbed out of the mud hole and stood in the sun. The mud hardened on them like ceramic armor, which they could crack off their bodies in big chunks. "The way a crab sheds its shell," said Pippa.

"A crab's shell comes off all in one piece," said Kim, who had been studying invertebrates in science class and felt pleased to remember what she'd learned.

Once the mud was cracked off and lying in pieces around them, they found that they were covered in dry, itchy dirt. "Too bad I can't put myself in one of Mr. Knuckles's washing machines," said Kimo, and even as the words were coming out, inspiration hit. He ran from the mud pond across the sand and straight down to the edge of the ocean, then he dove out into an oncoming wave. As the wave washed over him, he left a wide brown streak in the middle of it—like a signature.

"That's the coolest thing I've ever seen," Toby enthused, running after Kimo. Soon they were all in the ocean, laughing and splashing and washing off the mud. Then of course they had to do it all over again: the mud bath, the hairstyles, the face paint, the wrestling, the angels, the cracking dirt-armor, and the race into the waves, where they left long brown swirls. What a glorious morning!

They emerged from the ocean a couple of hours later, dripping saltwater. They stood in the hot sun and they all knew—at once—that they'd had just enough. They were ready to get going.

Tired, happy, their eyes rimmed with salt, they blinked and looked at each other. The mud might have come off their skin, but their clothes were a deep, dark brown.

"Good thing we're going to a laundromat," said Kim, and with that they headed away from the beach and back to the car.

CHAPTER
II

The first thing Kimo saw when they walked into the laundromat was one of the track-meet flyers pinned up over by the cash register, where Mr. Knuckles stood unrolling tubes of quarters and putting them into his cash drawer so he could make change for his customers. "Geez," said Kimo shyly. "Why'd you put that up?"

"Proud of you," Mr. Knuckles said.

"I haven't done anything yet," said Kimo.

"You will," said Mr. Knuckles. "You gonna crack dat record!"

This vote of confidence from Mr. Knuckles had the opposite effect on Kimo. Suddenly he felt nervous. What if he didn't break the record? What would Mr. Knuckles think of him then? "You're not coming to the meet, are you?"

"Sure," said Mr. Knuckles. "Yup. You a good kid, Kimo." The Fitzgerald-Trouts—all of them except for the baby—turned their heads and stared at Mr. Knuckles. In all the years they'd known him, he had never said anything like this. It was the kind of thing that a grown-up said, and Mr. Knuckles had never seemed much like a grown-up. Yes, he had tattoos. Yes, he owned an apartment and a business. But he had always acted like one of them. A friend, a buddy. He watched TV with them. He ate chocolate bars with them. He told jokes. And now here he was calling Kimo "a good kid."

"Are you sick?" Pippa pushed her glasses further up her nose.

"No," said Mr. Knuckles.

"Why'd you call him a kid?"

"He is kid," said Mr. Knuckles. Then, as if to brush off any further questions, he said, "Why you wet? Why you drip my floor?" (Mr. Knuckles spoke the language of the island fluently, but when he spoke English, he often left words out.)

"Mud." This was Toby.

"We found a big pond of it down by Pea Tree Beach," Kim clarified. Mr. Knuckles knew the spot exactly and explained to them how it had gotten there. The same big floods that had destroyed the Wildlife Safari Park all those months ago had washed silt down the mountain, forming a murky pond at the mountain's base. It had eventually evaporated until it was thick, glorious mud.

"You get dry clothes?" Mr. Knuckles asked. They nodded. "Okay, den. Use bathroom. Take off those. Wash 'em." Mr. Knuckles again sounded like a grown-up. "What you waiting for? Go."

Half an hour later they were dressed in dry clothes, seated on the laundromat's plastic chairs, watching sudsy piles of their dirty clothing go round and round in the washing machines. They were also watching their favorite soap opera, *Island Life*, on Mr. Knuckles's battered little TV. Though they hadn't watched an episode in many months, the plot seemed not to have advanced very much. Layla was still torn between which of the twins, Jack and Kai, she should marry. Jack and Kai were still angry with each other over who Layla loved the most. Layla's ex-boyfriend, Randolph, was still plotting to murder the twins.

"Wait," said Pippa. "The doc's going to put someone in a coma, which is a crime, so she can stop him from committing a crime?" Pippa loved the show precisely because it made no sense. Kim and Kimo loved it for the same reason—the characters in it behaved in such bizarre and incomprehensible ways. It was a source of endless bewilderment to them that the twins Kai and Jack would ever choose Layla over each other. They were siblings. Didn't they know what that meant?

Toby, who had Penny on his lap, wasn't interested in the show at all; for the same reason the others loved it, Toby found it boring. Who wanted to watch a bunch of stupid grown-ups doing stupid things? Instead he was flipping through one of Mr. Knuckles's surfing magazines. Toby's surf hero—Jackson Crunch—was killing it at Nationals and the photos of him shooting a tube were awe-inspiring. Penny had also plucked a magazine from the rack and was (literally) tearing through it, drooling and chewing on the pages as she went. When Toby saw this, he tried to take it away from her. But she clutched at it and shouted, "My do it!"

"No," he said. "These are for reading, not eating."

"My do it," the baby said again.

And that's when Toby saw what she was looking at: a photograph of herself.

My do it, indeed. The baby was in glossy color in the pages of the magazine. She was sitting on the grass, eating a picnic of baby food. When was Penny at a picnic? Toby wondered. And then it hit him like a dart: the grass wasn't grass; it was a backdrop. And the picnic wasn't a picnic; it was the photo shoot in Clarice's office. Above the baby's photograph in some kind of bubbly font was written the slogan *Because your baby loves Baby Loves.*

So Clarice had lied. The photographs of Penny weren't part of a contest. The photographs were advertisements to sell Clarice's Baby Loves products.

Toby quickly closed the magazine, only then noticing it was a copy of *Baby Loves Magazine.* Of course it was! He rolled it up tight and sat on it so that no one else would see it. The baby reacted to this betrayal, shrieking, "My! My!"

"Is she okay?" Kim had turned away from the TV to see what was going on.

"Yup," said Toby, tickling the baby's feet, deciding that he would not tell Kim—or the others—about the photograph. He knew that he hadn't done anything wrong by going with

Clarice; the baby had had fun and he had had fun. But the photo in the magazine, well, that was different. Clarice was using Penny's picture when Penny herself hadn't said it was okay. Not that Penny could talk. Still, Toby could talk, and he was Penny's older brother, and Clarice hadn't even asked for his permission to use the baby's picture. Toby was so immersed in his thinking that he barely noticed the chime of the laundromat's door, and it wasn't until he heard the others gasp that he realized it had opened and someone had come in.

That someone was Asha.

Only she didn't look much like Asha. To Toby, she looked like Asha if Asha had swallowed a small planet: Pluto, say, or even Venus.

"What's wrong with you?" The words were out of Toby's mouth before he could take them back.

"Nothing's wrong with her," said Kim. "Congratulations!"

"Thank you." Asha grinned.

"Why are you congratulating her?" Toby was

staring at Asha and remembering the time he'd blown too much air into a balloon and it had popped in his face. He turned to Mr. Knuckles. "You need to get her to a doctor."

"Doctor say she good." Mr. Knuckles was grinning from ear to ear and moving from behind the cash register to give Asha a kiss.

"Tobes," Pippa said, "Asha's going to have a baby. She's pregnant." Pippa turned to Asha. "Why didn't you tell us when we saw you the other day?"

"We only just started telling people, and I saw you at work," said Asha. Then she imitated her boss. "*No personal chit-chat on grocery store time.*"

"But we didn't even notice."

"The counter was blocking your view," said Asha.

"How could you block *that*?" Toby looked incredulous. "Do ladies always look that way when they get pregnant?"

Asha nodded and walked over to Toby so that her belly was at his eye level. "You want to feel her kick?"

"No thanks," said Toby. "Penny kicks me enough."

Everyone laughed at that, and then Kimo said, "Is it a girl? You said 'her.'"

"Yup," said Mr. Knuckles, straightening up and looking proud. It suddenly occurred to Kim that this was why Mr. Knuckles had been acting so strangely toward them earlier. He had treated them like kids because now that he was going to be a father, he felt like a grown-up.

"Her name right here," Mr. Knuckles said, pointing to a brand-new tattoo on his shoulder that said *Baby Girl*.

"That's cool," said Kimo. "But that's not actually her name."

"It is her name," Asha said. "Her father is insisting." Asha rolled her eyes a little and gave the Fitzgerald-Trout children a look that said *please talk some sense into him.*

"Um, Mr. Knuckles," said Kimo. "You absolutely cannot name a baby girl Baby Girl."

"Why not?"

"Because every baby eventually grows up, and someday your baby is going to be in sixth grade like me, and she won't want a name that will make her feel like a baby. And besides, *you* don't want her to have the name Baby Girl on her graduation diploma."

"Oh, right," said Mr. Knuckles, giving a small satisfied sigh at the thought of his unborn daughter someday graduating from elementary school.

Kimo gave Mr. Knuckles a thumbs-up, happy to have helped him make a good parenting decision. That's what I'm gonna do with my father, Kimo thought. When I break the pole vault record and he feels proud, then he will decide to give us the boat back and I will have made him a better dad. Kimo glanced at the flyer hanging above the cash register and it suddenly occurred to him that he had to make sure his father knew about the track meet. Otherwise, how would he know to show up?

"See, Hurley?" Asha was saying. "I knew they would be good to talk to about this." She looked at the children. "Didn't you guys name Penny?"

"We did," said Kim. "Well, Toby did." She told Asha that Toby's inspiration had been the words *Find a penny, pick it up, all day long you'll have good luck.*

"You know," said Asha, "you four are just about the best parents I've ever met in my life. You take great care of Penny. I don't know how you do it. We've been trying to get advice and reading a lot of magazines—there's one around here somewhere, that *Baby Loves Magazine* . . ."

She stooped down to search the magazine rack,

and Toby blurted out, "Forget the magazines. We can give you advice. Right, Penny? We know what we're doing."

"Mile," Penny said.

"She's saying that," said Toby, "because she's happy."

"See," said Asha. "That's exactly the kind of thing we need to know. How about as soon as the baby's born, we come to you for advice and you tell us everything you know about babies?"

"Yup," said Toby. He couldn't help feeling a sense of pride swelling in his chest. He'd always known a lot about taking care of his goldfish, but it was true, he knew a lot about taking care of his little sister too. Photo shoot or no photo shoot, he was a baby-care expert.

"We'd be happy to give you advice," said Kimo, who was busy formulating a plan about his own father. "The first few months are all about getting enough sleep for yourself while meeting the baby's basic needs."

"That's right," said Kim, but as she said it she felt a surge of unease. Should she be offering parenting lessons? Did she know anything at all about taking care of a baby? Now that she thought about it, Toby had been taking care of Penny much more than she had. When was the last time she'd sat down and really played with Penny or tickled her or talked to her? It was troubling to Kim that she couldn't remember. And then suddenly it wasn't troubling; Kim realized that she should be happy that she hadn't been tasked with taking care of Penny recently. She had done her fair share of baby care, when Toby was a baby and before that when the baby was Pippa. If she was watching Penny less, it was because she had earned the right to focus on her own work. Whatever else happened, Kim had to pass seventh grade and that wasn't going to happen if she got more Fs.

Pippa, for her part, was barely registering any of this. She was smiling at Asha and nodding her head, but what she was really thinking about was just how many pieces of scrimshaw she would have by the time Asha's baby was born, and she was asking herself if by then she would have told her siblings about her collection. She didn't know the answer to either of these questions.

"I'm counting on you," said Asha, then she pressed a hand to her belly. "I'm gonna go upstairs and make myself a cucumber, cream cheese, and raisin sandwich. You guys want one?"

Cucumber, cream cheese, and raisin? The children reluctantly nodded. It sounded awful, but they never said no to food.

Mr. Knuckles got to his feet. "Lemme help you," he said, following his wife out the back door of the laundromat. The music on the TV swelled. *Island Life* was back from commercial.

"I bet Layla decides to marry Jack but gets to the altar and realizes it's his twin, Kai," said Pippa, turning her attention to the TV.

"Good guess," said Kim. She noticed that the washing machines that held their clothes were done and got up to put the clothes in the dryer. Kimo followed her.

"I might go for a run," he said to Kim as he shoveled the wet laundry into a dryer.

"Thought you were taking a break today. No working out," said Kim.

"I was," said Kimo. "But that thing . . ." He nodded to the flyer hanging over the cash register. "There's a lot of pressure on me to break this record."

"I know," said Kim, "but you know it's okay either way. It's just cool that you've even gotten this close."

"Thanks," said Kimo, but as he said it, Kim saw something flash across his face, a shadow of an emotion that she didn't understand. She moved her nose up close to his nose, fixing her eyes on him. "Is that all that's bugging you? The track meet?"

"That's it," Kimo said, stepping back. He did not want Kim to know he was thinking about Johnny Trout. Kim, for her part, tried to follow the thread of his thoughts, the way that she had sometimes been able to do in the past, but she found she couldn't get anywhere.

"I'll meet you guys back at the Castle," Kimo said, then he ducked behind the cash register and took down the flyer.

"You running to the school?" Kim asked. "To use the track?"

"Maybe." Kimo shrugged, then he folded up the flyer and tucked it into his pocket. "I'll be back before dark," he said, running barefoot out the door.

He's being awfully mysterious, Kim thought. Then she wondered, where is he going?

CHAPTER
12

Swoosh, swoosh, went the blades of Kimo's kayak. His muscles ached pleasantly as he dug into the water and drove the nose of the thin blue boat forward through the waves. In front of him, the dark shadow of a lava gull played over the pale blue ocean. The curious gull was riding the breeze, lazily flapping its wings every minute or so. Kimo, on the other hand, was working hard, fighting offshore gusts that kept pushing the nose of the kayak out to sea. Using the foot pedals to guide the rudder, he aimed the boat parallel to shore. He was following the coastline, making his way from the downtown harbor—where he'd borrowed a kayak from Oshiro, the dockmaster—around the east side of the island to the little beach beneath the cliffs at Wabo Point.

The sun beat down on Kimo, who was working up a sweat. Every few strokes he would wipe the beads of moisture from his forehead with the back of his arm, then glance up at the lava gull. Man, look how effortlessly that gull is flying while I'm working my tail off, he thought. A bright light flashed in Kimo's eyes; he looked to see where it had come from and spotted a pod of dolphins riding the waves. Bursts of sunlight kaleidoscoped off their dorsal fins every time they leapt out of the water. Gulls, dolphins—everyone's taking it easy today. Only I am having a tough workout, Kimo thought with a frown. And then he laughed, thinking how neither the gull nor the dolphins would be attempting to break any records, but he would! That was why he was going where he was going—because of the track meet the following Saturday, because of the flyer that was folded into a tiny square and tucked into his pocket, because he wanted to invite his father, Johnny Trout—who had a cabin on the cliffs at the very end of Wabo Point—to the big event.

The coastline bent in and Kimo steered the kayak around the corner. He knew he was close to the Wabo cliffs because there were more lava gulls now, plummeting from the sky into the ocean, diving for their lunches. The gulls nested in the porous cliffs above the Wabo beach, and when Kimo and his siblings had—for a brief time—lived in Johnny Trout's cabin, they had watched the gulls hunt for fish and diligently carry them back to their nests to feed their chicks. During that time, Pippa had kept a notebook documenting the habits of the lava gulls, which she thought were excellent parents. *My dad should poke his head out of his cabin and take a few notes,* Kimo thought now. He could learn a thing or two from those birds. Maybe if he learned from them, I wouldn't have to teach him.

He felt his stomach grumble and he wished that he'd waited to take that cucumber, cream cheese, and raisin sandwich Asha had offered. Maybe when I get to the cabin my dad will give me some lunch, Kimo thought, then he laughed again. Kimo would be lucky if his dad's pet pig, Wendell, didn't try to eat *him* for lunch. Picturing his last encounter with Wendell—or, more precisely, with Wendell's teeth—Kimo had to ask himself, again, what the heck he was doing paddling out to Wabo Point. He definitely wouldn't break the island record for pole vaulting if he was in the hospital recovering from a pig attack. But I have to risk it, thought Kimo. I have to invite my dad.

As the kayak approached the beach, the gulls began to shriek, warning each other about the intrusion. The waves rolled him toward shore, so Kimo stopped paddling and swung his legs out of the boat. Then, when he was close, he jumped down into the shallow water, found his footing in the sand, and dragged the boat by its nose up onto the beach. A minute later he was grabbing the branches of the spice bushes that lined the path up the cliff and using them to propel himself up the steep incline. They released a wonderful smell, a mixture of nutmeg and cinnamon that made Kimo think of Christmas cookies. He knew that he was sweaty and that he probably smelled, and he hoped that the spice bushes would cover his scent so that Wendell wouldn't sniff him out. For the first time since he'd paddled out of the harbor, he felt grateful for the offshore breeze; the wind would carry his odor away from the cabin and the pig's nostrils.

But when he got to the top of the cliff there was no sign of the pig or of Johnny. They must be inside the cabin, he thought, and he crouched down, stealthing like a ninja through the tall grass toward the front door. When he got close, he saw that there was no car or truck parked near the cabin, so maybe Johnny wasn't home, which meant Wendell wasn't home (where Johnny went, the pig went). Kimo might be safe after all, but he wasn't taking any chances. He stayed low to the ground, crawling through a cloud of no-see-ums that he had to bat away so they wouldn't go into his eyes and mouth. Then he arrived at the side of the house where Johnny Trout had hung a wooden mermaid that had once been a ship's figurehead. "Hey, you," Kimo said, touching the peeling, faded paint on the mermaid's tail. "Long time no see."

Staying in a crouch, he moved to the window and pressed his face against the lower part of the glass. It was hard to see inside with the bright sunlight, so he shaded his eyes. If he squinted, he could just barely make out the shadowy features of the cabin's big front room. There was no indication that Johnny or the pig were home. Relaxing for the first time since he'd reached the top of the cliff, he exhaled and straightened up. He would take a look around.

Kimo knew the cabin would be locked, but he also knew that there was a little door cut into the back wall so that Wendell could go in and out as he pleased. He was happy to find that it had recently been widened to accommodate Wendell's increasing girth. Kimo just might be able to fit through the hole.

He got down on his knees and pushed the little door that hung from two hinges, then he put his hands together—like he was diving into water—and tucked his head between his arms. He shoved the front of his body, including his shoulders, through the opening. Now he was half in and half out. It occurred to him that if Johnny drove up at that moment, it would be hard to get loose quickly. He was likely to become a pig snack. The thought motivated him, and he pressed his hands against the floor, pulling himself forward while he wiggled his stomach and hips like a hula dancer. Slowly he hula-ed his way inside until he was lying flat in the middle of the kitchen floor, then he rolled over onto his back and jumped up to his feet like a gymnast.

The little kitchen was just as he remembered it, except for a new picture that Johnny had hung over the stove. It was a photograph of Johnny grinning on the bow of his sailing canoe, the *Mahina*. He was covered in leis—up to his ears—and holding a trophy because, as Kimo now remembered, Johnny had been awarded a prize for having completed the world's second-longest solo sea voyage. Beside Johnny stood Wendell.

The photograph was a reminder that Johnny and the pig could arrive home at any time. Kimo had better hurry. He swung open the fridge, where he discovered that one whole shelf was stocked with cans of guava juice. My father sure likes guava juice, he thought, taking out one of the cans and pressing it to his forehead to cool himself off. He let himself snap open the can and take a big, delicious drink. Someday I'll pay him back for this. And for these . . . he found himself grabbing a jar of almonds. Kimo really was quite hungry.

Munching on the nuts, sipping the juice, he padded toward the living room to try to find a good place to leave the flyer, some place where his father couldn't help but see it. Maybe the little desk in the cabin's bedroom would be the best spot. Johnny would be sure to notice it there.

Kimo ducked into the room and set his food down on the bookshelf. He took the flyer out of his pocket, unfolded it, smoothed it out, and placed it on top of Johnny's desk, near his typewriter, thinking, he's going to see this and he's going to come to the track meet and I'm going to break the world record and everything is going to change. Even as he was thinking this, Kimo saw that one of the flyers was already tacked on the bulletin board in front of Johnny Trout's desk. Yes, the very same flyer that Kimo had brought to leave on his father's desk was already there. Which meant that Johnny Trout cared enough about Kimo's track meet that he had kept the flyer and fastened it in a place where he would see it. Which meant that Johnny Trout wanted to be reminded of Kimo's track meet. Which meant that Johnny Trout was planning to come! It was too good to be true. Kimo's heart soared even as his ears registered the crunch of tires on gravel.

He moved to the window and peered out in the front of the house, where Johnny was just pulling up in his truck. For a brief instant Kimo wondered if he should just step outside and say hello to his father. After all, Johnny was planning on coming to his track meet; why not just say hi now and invite him in person. But then Kimo thought he probably shouldn't push his luck. Wendell didn't like him and any confrontation between Kimo and the pig might turn Johnny against Kimo. It might convince Johnny not to come to the track meet after all.

No, it was better to get out of there quickly and see his father on his own turf on Saturday. But he stood frozen, watching as Johnny opened the car door and stepped out, then held the door open for Wendell, who jumped out after him. Kimo did the math: the truck was approximately five strides from the front door, which meant that right about the moment when Johnny and the pig came through that door and entered the living room, Kimo would be coming through the door of the bedroom and entering the living room too. The pig would catch Kimo in the house unless Kimo could either stop time or move faster than the pig did.

Without another thought, Kimo dove out the door of the bedroom, landing like a cat on all fours, then he tucked into a ball and rolled across the floor. It was something he'd seen a ninja do in a movie, and it worked. He was up on his feet, charging across the kitchen as he heard the front door open.

"Come on, boy." Johnny was calling Wendell. "Come on . . ." There was a pause. "What's the matter?"

Wendell smells me, Kimo thought as he grabbed the handle of the back door and jerked it open. He hoped the pig was entering the house, not moving around outside it.

"Come on, boy. Inside," Johnny called again.

Kimo couldn't wait to find out whether the pig was headed in or staying out; he just had to run and hope. He jerked the door shut behind him and took off across the grass at a sprint, running for the cliff and the trail down to the water.

Threatened by his speed, certain he was coming for their chicks, a cloud of furious lava gulls began to dive at him. Kimo waved his arms in the air, batting them away as he dodged down the rocky path. They really are ferocious parents, Kimo thought, then smiled to himself. Maybe my dad will be too, someday.

It wasn't until a few minutes later, on the beach, catching his breath, that Kimo realized he had left the flyer on the desk. Johnny would certainly be surprised to see two of them. Would he know that

Kimo had left it? Would he be angry? Would he change his mind about coming to the meet? There was nothing Kimo could do but wonder as he pushed the kayak off the beach and began to paddle out of the cove.

CHAPTER

13

In the days that followed his visit to Johnny Trout's cabin, Kimo began to imagine what would happen if his father encountered his brother and sisters at the track meet. He knew how angry his siblings were with his father and he worried that they might confront Johnny and force him to leave before Kimo had a chance to break the record. If that happened, all Kimo's hard work would be for nothing.

So one night, as he and his siblings hiked up

the mountain to the Castle, Kimo said, with as much nonchalance as he could muster, "Hey, um, anyway, you guys don't have to come to my track meet."

"Of course we're going," said Kim, who was bouncing Penny on her shoulders, wondering when the little girl would ever walk or, at the very least, crawl.

"Go, go," said the baby.

"But you don't *have* to," Kimo tried again.

"We're going," said Pippa. "Duh."

"No," Kimo said abruptly. "You'll make me nervous if you come."

"We've never made you nervous before," Kim pointed out. She knew that something strange was going on, so she tried to look Kimo in the eye, but he avoided her, saying, "I think you might jinx my performance."

"Jinx?" snarked Pippa, offended.

"We're good luck," offered Toby.

Kim again tried to catch Kimo's eye, but he

wouldn't look at her, and she realized that he must have deliberately chosen to say all this as they were walking up the hill so that he didn't have to look at any of them. So she turned around and walked backward, facing him. "You can't be serious."

Kimo looked down at the ground. "I'm serious."

"Oh, come on," Kim said, trying a light tone. "We can't miss the big day. What if you break the record and we never see it?"

"What if I don't?" said Kimo. "I'll always think I was jinxed."

"But you *will* break it," said Toby, offering a vote of confidence.

"My do it!" shouted the baby, another voice of enthusiasm.

"You don't know that," Kimo said, then sighed. "Please, if you care about me, if you even *like* me, don't come to the track meet."

"What if I don't care about you or like you?" This was Pippa's idea of a joke.

"Then you won't want to be there anyway," reasoned Kimo.

"Good point," said Pippa.

They all lapsed into a silence that lasted until Kim began to chant, "Give a loud shout for Kimo Fitzgerald-Trout! He doesn't give up. He doesn't give in. He breaks the record, then breaks it again!" They all joined in and chanted until they reached the Castle.

Over the next few days, Kim did not give up on the issue of going to the track meet. Over and over again she nudged Kimo about it. Didn't he want to hear their cheering? Wouldn't it help him? She reminded him that they just wanted to be there; they didn't care if he broke the record or not. Over and over Kimo thought of his father coming to the track meet and insisted it would be unlucky to have his brother and sisters there. Finally, begrudgingly, they promised to stay away.

But Kim wasn't able to keep her promise

entirely. She had a science fair project to do, which had moved to the top of her to-do list (it was due several days before her speech on table manners), so she decided she would research the birds that lived in the mushimush trees in the school's courtyard—and that way she would be there, at the school, researching, while Kimo was at the track attempting to break the island record.

Now on the Saturday morning of the track meet, Kim lay in the grass beneath the trees; she was close enough to the track to hear the crowd gathering for the meet. Though she was looking up at the mushimush branches through a pair of binoculars and had her notebook open to her research, her mind was entirely on Kimo. I'm right here, she thought. And Kimo, my almost-twin, is just across the field. Soon he will be like one of these birds. He'll be up in the air and he'll either fly over the bar and break the record or he won't.

Kim felt that she had to be there—at the track—to see what happened, but she had promised to stay away. Then she realized that she held in her hands the perfect tool to do both: binoculars. What if she climbed one of the trees? What if she watched from there? Surely that wouldn't be a jinx.

Kimo could feel the ocean breeze on his face as he slowly turned the corner of the track. He was warming up as he always did, with a slow two-mile run that would be followed by a series of quicker sprints and then some stretches. As he ran, he took stock of the day's conditions. It was hotter than he liked—he would have to have a few sips of water before his jump—but there was a breeze, and that was a good thing. A strong breeze off the ocean meant wind at his back during his sprint to the vault. That wind might just be the little extra push he needed to clear the fifteen-foot-and-two-inch mark that stood between him and the record.

He could hear the car tires crunching in the school's parking lot, and he could see people pouring across the field, through the gates, and up the stairs into the bleachers that lined the long side of the track. He tried not to look up into those stands, where many of the seats were already full and vendors were selling Uncle Ozo's soda pop and salty fried clams served in rolled up cones of newspaper. They don't usually sell clams at track meets, Kimo thought, and that's when it occurred to him just what an island-wide event his record-breaking attempt had become. The thought of this excited Kimo. The crowds would be encouraging. Like the breeze, they would lift him up and over the high bar. He wondered if his father had arrived yet, but he decided not to check. There would be time later—after the track meet ended and before the big jump—to scan the bleachers for his father's gnarled and bearded face. He picked up his pace and began the sprinting part of his warm-up.

As he ran, he started to wish his brother and sisters were there to watch him. Boy, what he wouldn't give to be able to see their smiling faces. He knew they were hurt that he'd told them not to come to the meet, but despite their hurt, that morning Kim had insisted on driving him to the school, and Pippa and Toby had decided to walk down the mountain to see him off. As they'd walked, they had chanted: "Give a loud shout for Kimo Fitzgerald-Trout! He doesn't give up. He doesn't give in. He breaks the record, then breaks it again!" When they got to the little green car, Pippa, Toby, and the baby had all given Kimo hugs and wished him luck. Then they waved as Kim had driven Kimo off to his date with destiny.

What Kimo and Kim didn't know was that on the way back uphill, Pippa had realized that she could do some scrimshaw-hunting on her own if she could just get Toby to stay at the Castle with the baby. So as soon as they got within sight of the leafy structure, she had said, with a practiced nonchalance, "I feel like taking a longer hike. You wanna come?"

"Nope," said Toby. Pippa had known this would be his response. Her younger brother could always be counted on to choose daydreaming over exercise. As she turned onto the path away from the Castle, Pippa offered to take Penny with her, but the baby was already trying to get off her shoulders.

She was reaching for Toby, saying, "Mile."

"What's she talking about?" Pippa asked.

"Who knows?" said Toby, lifting the baby off Pippa and then, careful not to break the spider's web, ducking through the Castle door.

And so it was that while Kimo warmed up on the track and Kim watched him through the binoculars and Pippa scoured the mountain for another piece of scrimshaw, Toby found himself sitting in the moss, trying to teach Penny to crawl. "Crawl," he said. "Come on, Penny, crawl."

The baby didn't move, but she repeated, "Quall," and let loose a long string of drool from her mouth.

"Like this," said Toby, getting down on all fours and showing the baby how to do it.

"Looks like fun," a woman's voice said from somewhere near the Castle door. Toby, whose back was to the door, noticed that Penny was smiling.

"Wimo," the baby said, informing Toby with a single word just who was standing in the doorway. Clarice. But how did she know where to find him? Then Toby remembered in a flash that the last time he'd seen Clarice, he had told her where they lived.

"I've got an idea," Clarice was saying. She was wearing high heels and leaning up against the stone doorway, feeling around for something in her purse.

How did she get up the mountain in those

stupid shoes? Toby wondered, but what he said was, "Yeah? What?"

Clarice didn't answer for a moment. She was busy trying to find the thing in her purse, peering down into the bag. It looked to Toby like whatever her idea was, she thought it might be buried next to her wallet and lipstick. At last, Clarice found what she was looking for and pulled it out: a nail file. She leaned back and began to file her nails. So now Toby knew Clarice wasn't even trying to break the island record for longest fingernails; she was, in fact, purposefully shortening her nails. For some reason this annoyed the boy, and he blurted out, "Well, what? Just say it already."

"This place you're living in." Clarice was taking her time. "I can see the appeal. It's spacious and well-situated. Good view. But the truth is, it could use some work. You need furniture and window-panes, not to mention a roof and a floor."

"Who says?" Toby was defensive. He liked the Castle just the way it was. But Clarice wouldn't understand that. She was wearing high heels that were sinking down into the moss. Anyone wearing shoes on moss would never understand the charm of a house where trees grew through open windows.

Clarice must have picked up on this because now she said, "Maybe you like it this way, but even so, there must be things that you want to make it better . . ."

Toby shrugged indifferently, but he couldn't help thinking about the things he *did* want. To start with, he'd like a wall around his room with a door cut into it. That would make his space entirely his. And now that he thought about it, his brother and sisters probably wanted things too. He knew Kim had been talking nonstop about table manners and how if they were ever going to learn any, they needed to have a real table. And Pippa talked constantly about how she wanted a proper way to hang her knickknack shelf on the Castle's stone walls (it now hung from the branch of a tree). And hadn't Kimo just the other day said that it would be nice to have a chin-up bar? "Maybe there are things," Toby admitted.

"I knew it," Clarice said with a smile, that tight-lipped smile that made her look like a snake. "That's why I'm here. If you scratch my back, I'll scratch yours."

Toby looked at her fingernails and understood that that was why she was filing them down. "I don't care how short your nails are," he said. "I don't want to be scratched."

This made Clarice laugh. "It's a figure of speech," she said. "I wouldn't really scratch you. I just mean, if I help you make this place better, then you'll help me, right?"

"Help you how?"

"I'd like to take Penny."

"And take pictures of her, like you did last time? And make an advertisement?" Toby was not going to be fooled by this woman again.

"Oh, you saw that," Clarice said.

"Yup." Toby had his arms crossed over his chest angrily. "You should have been honest with me. You said it was a contest, but it wasn't. You just bought me a lot of food while you took those pictures of Penny for your baby magazine."

"You're right." Clarice put away the nail file. "I should have been honest with you. And that's why I'm being honest now. If you let me take Penny to do another advertising shoot, then I'll pay you enough money to fix up this place."

"Let me think about it," said Toby. He noticed for the first time that Clarice had broken the spiderweb which hung in the doorway. Toby and his siblings had always ducked under it as a sign of respect to the spider, but Clarice hadn't done that; she'd just shoved right through it and destroyed the spider's home. She was a thoughtless person. Something Toby wasn't going to be. "I need to talk to my brother and my sisters," he said.

"All right," said Clarice, adding, "How soon can you talk to them?"

"Not soon," said Toby, glancing over at Goldie in his jar that sat on one of the fireplaces.

"Too bad," said Clarice. "I guess it won't work out then."

"Why?" Now Toby hesitated. He didn't want to miss the chance to do something good for the others, like fixing up the Castle.

"I need to do this photo shoot today. Benicio's arriving at my office any minute." Clarice turned to go. "I bet your brother and sisters would have liked to have a nicer place to live."

Toby looked down at Penny, who was holding her arms out to Clarice like she wanted to be picked up.

"I think she likes my offer," Clarice said, pointing at the baby.

"She likes your car," said Toby. Then he said, "How much money would you give us?"

Clarice waved into the air vaguely. "Enough to repair this dump completely."

"A hundred dollars," said Toby. It sounded like

a large sum to him, and he figured they'd be able to do all the fixing up that they wanted with that much money.

"Fine," said Clarice, frowning at the baby but reaching down to pick her up.

"I'll carry her," said Toby.

"Oh," said Clarice. "You don't need to come with us."

"Are you kidding?" Toby almost shouted. "Of course I'm coming with you. I'm not letting her go on her own."

Clarice grimaced and didn't say anything. She seemed to be reconsidering the whole plan, but she shrugged and said, "Fine. All right. But hurry along, I don't have all day." She turned away, then added, "And don't bring that goldfish. He's too much trouble."

This infuriated Toby, but he thought that if he contradicted Clarice, she might just decide he wasn't invited after all. He glanced over at Goldie. Sorry, he thought, because he knew Goldie could hear his thinking. I'll be back soon. He grinned at the fish, but Goldie did not smile back at him. Toby knew Goldie was thinking that what Toby was about to do was a very bad idea. Again, Toby hesitated. Should he listen to his friend? He let out a large sigh and made his decision. He had to go with Clarice. He had to make the Castle better. For everyone.

Patting the lid of the jar as if he were patting the fish on the back, he thought, When I get that money, I'll get you a bigger jar. He looked away before Goldie could think anything else at him, and he scooped up Penny, lifting her onto his shoulders. He would carry her down the mountain to the parking lot, where he was sure Leon would be waiting in the limousine to take them to the Royal Palm hotel. What Toby couldn't know was that Clarice had no intention of going to the hotel because she had an entirely differ-ent destination in mind, because she had an entirely different plan for Penny.

CHAPTER
14

Kimo planted his pole in the pit and stepped back to measure just exactly where his foot would need to be for the pole to land properly, then he turned to walk backwards up the track, counting his steps. He had done this many times before; he knew that there were seventeen strides from the top of the track to the spot where he would plant the pole and then flip himself up into the air and over the bar. He had been visualizing his run for days, and he pictured it again now as he walked up to the top of the track where Ms. Bonicle was standing waiting for him. All the other pole-vaulters had already gone. It was Kimo's turn.

The bar was set at fifteen feet, two inches, the new island record. If Kimo went over it, he would not only be the island record holder but the young-est island record holder ever! Was it too much to hope for?

The bleachers were packed with faces: some had smiling mouths, some had talking mouths, and some had mouths full of fried clams that Kimo could smell wafting on the breeze, a breeze that would help him with his run down the track. As he walked up the track, counting his seven-teen strides, he let his eye run along the row of faces of the people seated in the front row of the bleachers. No bearded man, no Johnny Trout. His father wasn't in the bottom row. He ran his eye along the second row of bleachers—there were two bearded men, but neither of them was Johnny. He did this for the third, fourth, and final rows of the bleachers, but to no avail. His heart clenched and his gut churned like there were snakes in his stomach as he realized that his father was not in the crowd.

Someone shouted his name from the top row: "Ki-mo! Ki-mo!" He turned to see Mr. Knuckles and Asha waving to him. Then a group of students who Kimo knew from his class took up the chant, calling out, "Ki-mo, Ki-mo, Ki-mo, Ki-mo." Others joined in, and by the time Kimo took the last stride into his spot at the top of the track, the whole crowd was shouting his name. Kimo waved and smiled and the snakes in his belly dissolved. He felt a surge of happy possibility. How he wished his brother and sisters were watching and cheering. There had been no point in keeping them away, since Johnny Trout hadn't come.

"Are you ready?" Ms. Bonicle had to shout into Kimo's ear to be heard over the noise of the crowd. Kimo thought about his father and wondered if he should wait. What if Johnny showed up right after Kimo had jumped?

"One more minute," Kimo said.

Ms. Bonicle nodded, then hollered into his ear again. "Take your time. Enjoy this." She meant the encouraging shouts of the crowd. Kimo smiled again, but inside he wasn't smiling. He was thinking about Johnny. Where was his father now? He's probably tossing meatballs to that pig of his and watching the pig jump in the air. He's probably forgotten all about my jump. "You've got natural ability and you've worked hard," his coach was yelling. "Just do your best. *Swish, swish, pop, zow-wee!* Remember?"

"I remember," Kimo said. Now or never, he said to himself, stepping away from his coach and into the spot where he would begin. He lifted the pole up into position. As if the pole were a wand casting a spell, the crowd fell into a hush. No one said a word. Even the birds had stopped singing. I wish Kim was here, Kimo thought. I wish Pippa and Toby and Penny were here. But he chased these thoughts into the back of his mind.

He took a deep breath and began to run. Keeping his knees high, he sprinted toward the bar. One, two, three, four . . . he was counting his strides to the spot where he would plant the pole. Five, six, seven, eight, nine, ten, eleven, twelve, thirteen, fourteen . . . a man emerged from the parking lot and stood at the gate. Even as he ran, Kimo registered the man's grimacing, unpleasant face, framed by a shaggy beard. Fifteen, sixteen, seventeen . . . it was Johnny Trout, standing right there. My father came to see me break the record . . . as Kimo had this thought, he forgot to plant his pole in the pit. By the time he remembered, his pole was so far forward that he launched himself into the space directly under the high bar.

There was nothing he could do to stay out of the way of the bar. Nothing he could do to clear fifteen feet, two inches.

The bar was knocked from its rest.

The crowd gave a groan as Kimo tumbled down onto the foam mat and the bar fell down on top of him. The record was not broken.

Embarrassed, Kimo lay there, staring up at the sky, where clouds trundled past, indifferent to his loss. His nostrils flared as furious thoughts swirled in his head. He was angry with his father for showing up just then and distracting him, but he was even angrier with himself for losing focus.

The very thing that he had hoped his father would see—the highest pole vault ever—had been destroyed by his father's arrival.

Why had he invited his father in the first place? He felt tears squeezing out of his eyes as into his blurry view stepped Johnny Trout.

"Hey, kid," the old pirate said.

"Hi." Kimo's voice wavered. He wiped his eyes with the back of his hand.

"You didn't break the record," Johnny said.

"No," said Kimo, sitting up on the foam mat and looking at Johnny. He felt then that if his father said even one kind thing, everything would be okay and it would all be worth it: all the training, even the humiliation of failing to break the record would be worth it for this chance to talk to his father face-to-face. "No, I didn't," Kimo said.

"People said you were good at this pole vaulting thing." Johnny shrugged. "Boy were people wrong. My pig could jump higher than you did."

So that was it. What a terrible thing to say. Kimo watched his father turn and start back toward the gate that was crowded with people returning to their cars in the parking lot. He wanted to shout something at his father, something about how he was absolutely sure no pig on earth could jump fifteen feet, two inches. But what would be the point of calling out Johnny's absurd brag about his pet?

And that was when Kim appeared. She had seen it all from her perch in the trees and she wanted to tell Johnny how hard Kimo had worked and how good he was at pole vaulting and that the only reason he hadn't broken the record was because Johnny had ruined his attempt. But when she stepped in front of Johnny and poked her finger into the part of Johnny's chest where his heart would have been if he'd had a heart and opened her mouth, nothing came out. Nothing.

She opened and closed her mouth again. She felt strangled, her words cut off. Her head was whirling, and she remembered her teacher telling her that to become good at public speaking, she would need to practice. This is practice, she thought, but still no words emerged.

Johnny was staring at her with an amused look on his face. After a minute he said, "Cat got your tongue?"

"Doesn't . . . cat . . . no," Kim squeaked.

Johnny laughed and shouted loudly enough that a couple of people stopped to watch. "You need somebody to do your talking for you. Where are the others? There's never just one of you brats." He scanned the crowd filing out of the gate. "Where's the one with the freckles and the temper? She's good at yelling. Or the goldfish boy? Or that shrimp with no teeth?"

She's a baby, Kim wanted to say, and she has three teeth. But instead of the words rushing out of her, she felt *worry* rushing *into* her. She realized that she didn't know exactly where the others were. An alarm began to sound deep inside her, an alarm that said, You need to find the others. You need to know where they are. But she didn't have time to register this alarm because Johnny was saying, "I can't wait to get my hands on that boat. I'm sure it'll be mine soon." He gave a big grin and started off.

Watching him leave, Kim felt the worry and the words combine into a force so powerful that they did finally explode out of her. And the words that came out were, "Napkin in your lap and elbows off the table!"

Just at the moment she had hoped to chastise Johnny Trout for his treatment of Kimo, she found herself instead shouting some of the words about table manners that she had memorized for her speech.

Johnny Trout didn't even turn to look at her; he just walked away. It was utterly humiliating.

But then she looked over and saw Kimo sitting

slumped on the foam mattress and she understood that her own humiliation was nothing compared to what he had just been through in front of the crowd at the track meet. "He ruined your chances." Kim plopped down on the mattress next to him.

The boy looked over at her. "I thought if I jumped well, if I broke the record, he'd be proud of me and maybe, just maybe, he'd give us our boat back."

"No matter how high you jumped, he would never do that," said Kim. "He's too terrible. You can't change him."

"I thought I could," said Kimo.

"That's because you could never be terrible," Kim said, getting to her feet. "So you can't even imagine someone like him." She noticed how easy it was to speak now that her audience was just her brother. She pulled him to his feet and folded him into a hug. "You'll try again," Kim said. "And next time we'll be there to give you good luck."

Kimo could see Ms. Bonicle standing at the top of the track talking to one of the other coaches. He knew he should go and talk to her, but he didn't feel up to it yet. "Thanks for *trying* to yell at him," Kimo said.

"Where's Pippa when you need her?" asked Kim, and that's when she finally registered the alarm that Johnny Trout's words had set off deep inside her. Where IS Pippa? she thought. "We have to go find her," Kim said. "I'm worried that something's happened."

Still regretting his decision not to have invited the others, Kimo agreed they should return to the Castle right away. He wanted to put this day behind him by hanging out with his siblings.

But when they emerged from the woods near the Castle, only Pippa was waiting for them. She was pacing back and forth, wearing a path through the moss. "Hey," Kimo shouted. "We're home."

Pippa looked up at them and Kim saw from the

expression on her sister's face that she was worried. "Everything okay?" Kim asked.

"Toby and Penny," Pippa said, her eyes wide open, her mind reeling with awful possibilities. "They're gone."

CHAPTER
15

W hcre did they go?" Kim shook her head in disbelief.

"That's the thing." Pippa's voice cracked, and the freckles on her face seemed to throb. "I don't know. I just got back a couple minutes ago." Kim noticed that the little girl's glasses were fogging up. Kim couldn't remember ever having seen Pippa cry.

"I'm sure they're fine," said Kimo. "Just swimming or picking guavas or something."

But Pippa shook her head and slide her backpack off. She reached into it and pulled out two pieces of bone. She held them out to Kim and Kimo and explained that they were scrimshaw from Captain Baker's collection. She told the story of finding the first piece and then deciding she needed more. She confessed that she had been slipping off at night. "I was lying," she said, putting her face in her hands.

"Now you've told us," said Kim. "You've come clean."

"I guess I see why you kept them a secret," said kindhearted Kimo. "They're beautiful. You wanted to have something all your own. Don't worry about it."

"But Penny and Toby . . ." Pippa trailed off. "They've disappeared and it's my fault."

"None of this means anything has happened to them." Kimo patted his little sister on the shoulder. "They'll be back."

"No," Pippa said. "I didn't tell you the worst

part." And then she told about the prints she'd found—the scythe-shaped prints—that belonged to the monster, the rustling monster. "I should have said something," Pippa choked out. "What if the monster's taken Toby and the baby?" Pippa pointed at the door to the Castle. "The web's broken," she said. "Toby wouldn't break the web."

And that is when Kim's heart stopped in her chest. She knew that what Pippa had said was true. "What have I done? What have I done?" Kim pressed her face into her hands, then looked up and spoke in a whisper. "Do you think that a ghost can make rustling noises and leave footprints?"

"A ghost?"

"People say that Captain Baker's ghost roams the mountain. I read it in my textbook. I didn't tell you guys 'cause I didn't want you to want to leave the Castle."

Pippa and Kim stood there in horror, imagining Toby and Penny in the clutches of a rustling, scythe-footed ghost until Kimo very reasonably said, "How can a ghost leave footprints? Ghosts are made of air or ghost dust or slime or something."

"I don't even think that I believe in ghosts," said Kim. "But *something* made the noises that we heard."

"And something left the prints," Pippa said, staring down at her own feet.

"Wizzleroaches," Kimo said, uttering the name of the thing that frightened him most.

"Wizzleroaches don't leave big prints," said Kim. "They don't have big feet."

"Don't talk about their feet!" Kimo shouted, already getting that creepy-crawling feeling in his belly.

"Okay," said Kim, trying to reason through things calmly. "All right. Let's talk about other feet. If Toby and Penny were taken by something, then there would be prints around here, wouldn't there?" Without another word, the children examined the floor of the Castle, looking for more prints, but the moss was so spongy that if any monster had walked there, no prints showed.

"Maybe there are some outside," Kim said, already heading back to the door, and that's when she saw something that made her scream. Pippa saw it too. It was Goldie, sitting in his jar on one of the fireplaces. Now they knew for certain that something was terribly wrong, because if Toby were just picking guavas or swimming or anything else, he would have taken the goldfish with him. They raced to the door of the Castle to begin searching for more prints, but as they headed out of the house and into the woods that surrounded it, they saw a figure on the other side of the purple field of orchids.

It was a little boy in shorts and a torn T-shirt, emerging from the distant trees. They recognized those shorts and they knew that T-shirt. Both belonged to Toby. But the face was not quite Toby's face. It was too pale and too shaken. It was, in a word, ghostly. And that's when Kim, Kimo, and Pippa all had the same thought—that the rustling ghost-monster had taken Toby and devoured him and that what they were looking at was *Toby's ghost*.

Without hesitation, Kim proclaimed, "Ghost or not, he's still our brother." Kimo and Pippa clearly agreed because they all charged across the field at a sprint. But when they got to Toby, they found that he was not a ghost at all. He was a real, live boy, and he was very scared. Between gulps of air, he told them that he'd been on the other side of the island, that something awful had happened, that he'd gotten a ride back to the mountain, and that he had run all the way up it in hopes of finding them. "Come on," he said breathlessly, pulling at their hands. "We have to go now! We have to run!"

"We're just glad you're okay," Kimo said, throwing his arm around Toby and pulling him close. "We thought you'd been snatched by a monster."

"No," Toby said. "Not me, but—" And even before he could speak, the older siblings knew what he was going to say, because they were looking around, realizing that the baby wasn't there. "She's got Penny."

"The rustling scythe-footed ghost-monster?" asked Pippa.

"No," said Toby. "Clarice McGuffin. She's got a lawyer. She's signing legal papers. If we don't stop her, she's going to become Penny's mother."

CHAPTER
16

Grrrg, grrrg, grrrrg, clunk. The engine of the little green car would not start. Sitting in the driver's seat, feeling helpless, Kim turned the key once more. *Grrrg, grrrg, grrrrg, clunk.* No luck. She banged her fist on the steering wheel in frustration. She needed to get the engine going so they could rescue Penny, who was somehow now being held by the CEO of Baby Loves. Kim didn't understand what had happened. All Toby had managed to explain as they'd run down the mountain to the car was that Clarice had offered money to fix the Castle up if he and Penny went with her to photograph something.

"Wait," Kimo said. "How does Clarice even know Penny? Or you? Or where we live?" Toby backed up his story and hurriedly admitted that he'd met Clarice before and that he'd accidentally told her where they were living. Then he confessed, "One time, after school, while you guys were busy, I went with Penny to Clarice's office at the Royal Palm hotel. Penny had her picture taken for *Baby Loves Magazine* while I ate room service." On a normal day Pippa and Kimo would have asked what room service was, but this wasn't a normal day.

Toby groaned, then explained the rest of what he knew. "Clarice doesn't care about Penny. She's trying to adopt her so she can take her picture anytime she wants and use it for advertisements."

Hearing this, Kim began to beg the little green car. "Start, please, start. Please!" She twisted the key, and her wish was answered. The engine sputtered to life.

"Yes!" they all yelped in chorus. The car didn't sound energetic, but it was running. Kim threw it into reverse and backed out of the parking space, turning to Toby to ask, "Where exactly are we going?"

"Island Record Studios."

"Where's that?" Kimo asked as Kim pulled out onto the main road.

"It's a giant warehouse," said Toby, "in the middle of that bamboo grove near Barber Street."

"Wait," Pippa interjected. "I thought you said Clarice's place was at the Royal Palm hotel."

"That's the thing," said Toby. "This time we didn't go to her office. This time we went to *Tina's* office."

The name struck the Fitzgerald-Trout siblings like a dart. "Tina!" Pippa howled in fury. "Our mother Tina?" Toby's head tucked between his shoulders like a turtle disappearing into its shell.

Pippa was ranting now. "Tina who sings jingles about Baby Loves but doesn't love her own baby? That Tina?"

Toby had never been so miserable. "I heard Clarice asking Tina to sign the papers so that Baby Loves could adopt Penny."

"Baby Loves? The corporation?" asked Kimo.

Kim wailed loudly and pushed the gas pedal, but it was already to the floor. The little green car was going as fast as it possibly could (which was not very fast at all).

Toby's face twisted into a grimace. "Tina said, 'Sure, why not? Baby Loves can have her.'" Pippa's jaw dropped open and Kimo clutched his heart while Kim's hands began to shake; it was all that she could do to keep the car pointing straight.

"And what about Clive?" Kimo asked. He knew of course that Clive had always been a terrible father, but the boy held out hope that Clive might at least not want a corporation to own his baby.

Toby shook his head. "Clarice asked about

Clive, and Tina told her that Clive's already signed over full custody because he's 'allergic' to Penny." Toby made the air- quotes with his hands and the other Fitzgerald-Trouts all shook their heads in disbelief, not over the fact that Clive was a terrible parent—*that* they knew—but over the fact that he could ever think Penny gave him allergies. It was ridiculous.

For a long moment none of them said anything. Kim slowed the car as a cloud of coral-colored flamingos, awkward as a flock of umbrellas, flew past. When the flamingos were gone, Toby said, "I snuck out. I told Leon, he's Clarice's limo driver, what had happened and I asked him for a ride back to Mount Muldoon so I could get you guys."

"Why did you do that?" Kim couldn't help herself. She was yelling at Toby. "Why not get the limo driver to help you take Penny back?"

"I asked him," wailed Toby. "I did. But he said he couldn't help me take Penny. No grown-up could help. That would be kidnapping."

"They're the ones who are kidnapping," Pippa said, her freckles flaring. She felt a surge of anger at Tina and then a surprising anger at Toby. She should have known better than to trust him with the baby. He was an irresponsible daydreamer. Then she felt a deep blush of shame; at least Toby had been with the baby. She couldn't say the same for herself. She took her glasses off and rubbed them on her ratty T-shirt as calmly as she could. "So let me get this straight. Tina is filling out papers so that Clarice's corporation can adopt Penny. And Clarice is probably paying Tina a lot of money. Is that what's happening?"

"Yup," said Toby. "When I left, Clarice was calling her lawyer to come over." He was anxiously picking the stuffing from a hole in the seat next to him.

"How can a corporation take care of a baby? A corporation isn't a person." In his distress, Kimo started opening and closing the glove compartment as if he might find an answer there.

Kim's question was different. "How can Tina give Penny away? She's not Tina's baby. She's our baby." Even as she said this, Kim was realizing how little attention she'd paid to the baby lately. And earlier this afternoon she hadn't known where Pippa was and that was partly because Kimo hadn't wanted them all at the track meet. Their little family unit had come apart, blown in different directions like the seeds of a dandelion. Only we did it to ourselves, Kim thought. It wasn't the wind that scattered us.

"We know she's our baby," Pippa said. "But do they know it?"

"We're gonna go there and tell them." Kim slapped her palm against the steering wheel, a gesture of angry resolve. "We're going to get our sister back. Simple as that."

They drove as quickly as they could to Island Record Studios, but when they got there, things were not as simple as Kim had hoped. For one thing, the large metal doors to the windowless warehouse were locked. Kimo yanked on them with all his might, but they seemed to be bolted from the inside. "Is this how you got in before?" he asked Toby.

"It's how I got out too."

Pippa was clenching and unclenching her fists, preparing for some kind of battle. "I bet they noticed you'd left and they figured you were going for help and they locked the doors up tight."

Kim stared up at the impenetrable warehouse. There were no other doors, no open windows, and the building was flanked on both sides by tall, tangled groves of bamboo. "How are we ever going to get inside?"

Pippa stepped back several yards and squinted up at the building. It had occurred to her that if she could find a way for all of them to get into it, she would in some small way make up for the mistake of having left Toby and the baby alone. Her eyes scanned the structure for evidence of entry points. There were the doors, bolted from the inside, and several high windows that looked permanently sealed. What about the roof? She walked a few paces back to get a better look and that's when she saw a large metal hatch that could only be one thing. "There's an air-conditioning unit up there," she said, pointing to the rooftop.

"So?" Kimo was impatient.

"If it breaks, somebody has to be able to get up there to fix it," said Pippa. "Which means there's got to be an opening on the roof—a door or something—that leads into the building."

"But there's no way to get up there." Toby groaned. "It's way too high."

"Maybe we could climb the bamboo," said Pippa. But when they reached the edge of the bamboo that grew densely beside the building, they saw that the distance from the top of the bamboo to the roof was much too great.

A frightening thought occurred to Kim. "Maybe Tina and Clarice aren't even in there. Maybe they saw that Toby was gone and they took Penny to meet the lawyer somewhere else."

But a quick survey of the cars in the parking lot revealed Tina's blue convertible parked across from Clarice's limo. So the two women had to still be inside the building. "Where's that limousine driver you were telling us about?" Pippa turned to Toby. "Maybe he knows a way in."

"Leon," said Toby. "He gave me a ride to the mountain. Dunno where he is now. I guess he could be inside. Sometimes when he's not driving, he watches TV."

"So he's no help." Kim was pacing and blowing air out of her cheeks in furious puffs. "How long does it take to draw up adoption papers? Maybe the lawyer's not here yet. Maybe when she gets here—"

"Why do you think she's a she?" asked Toby. "Boys can be lawyers too."

This was the kind of unnecessary digression from Toby that drove Kim crazy, but instead of snapping at her little brother, she reminded herself that he was the one who had been paying the most attention to the baby lately. He had been taking care of Penny when Kim had been too busy with her own pursuits. "You're right," said Kim, correcting herself. "Maybe when she—or he—gets here, we can slip into the building with her—or him."

"He's a he," said Pippa. "And he's already here." She had been studying the cars in the parking lot and was pointing to one with the personalized license plate MR LAWMAN. "That's gotta be his car—which means the papers could already be signed."

Kim's blood ran cold. "We've got to get in there now and tear those papers up or burn them or at least snatch them away."

"They'll just write up another set," wailed Toby.

Kimo was not going to hear this kind of hopeless talk. "We have to think of a way to get in because when we get in, we'll know just what to do, because we have to know what to do or we'll lose Penny for good."

Pippa was not going to be defeated. "If we can cut a path through the bamboo, we can get around to the back and see if there's a door there on the other side. Do we still have that ax in the trunk?" They found it, and a moment later, Kimo was charging toward the bamboo grove.

But as he charged toward it, Kimo heard a familiar sound. It was a sound that made his palms sweat and his heart race. It was a sound that made him itch all over. It was the sound of wizzleroaches—or, more specifically, wizzleroach *feet*. Because all of the wizzleroaches that fled Mount

Muldoon when the lava had come had found a new home in the bamboo grove on Barber Street. And now Kimo was charging straight into them. But to the great surprise of Kimo's siblings—and of Kimo himself—he did not stop. His fear of losing Penny was much greater than his fear of the insects, and so he ran right into their midst, swinging the ax at the bamboo stalks as if his life depended upon it. The other children watched in awestruck silence. Clouds of the wizzleroaches flew past Kimo, but he kept swinging, he kept moving, deeper and deeper into the bamboo grove. He didn't miss a stroke.

Still, as strong as he was and as great as his effort was, he made slow progress. After several restless minutes Pippa said, "I can't just stand here doing nothing. I'm going to watch the door to the building and make sure no one's going in or out. It would be ridiculous if someone happened to open the door and we weren't there."

"Good plan," said Kim.

"Do it," Kimo huffed between strokes of the ax.

Pippa took off and Toby and Kim resumed watching Kimo work. After a minute, Kim noticed that Kimo had only cut a small fraction of the trail that would need to be thirty or forty feet long before it cleared the side of the building. "This could take all day." She shook her head, then offered, "Let me have a turn."

"No," said Kimo.

"You're slowing down," said Kim. "I'm not slowing down."

"Yes, you are," said Toby gravely.

Kimo heard the boy's tone and gave in, stepping aside and handing the ax off to Kim, who immediately raised it over her shoulder and began to hew away the next few feet of bamboo.

Kimo bent to clear the stalks that he had already cut. He picked up a few and carried them out of the grove into the parking lot. As he emerged, Pippa, who was standing near the front door, had a view of him from a distance. It looked to her like he was carrying a couple of pole-vaulting poles and this made her realize she didn't even know if he'd broken the island record or not. "Hey," she shouted. "How did it go at the track meet?"

"Not good," said Kimo.

"Well," said Pippa, "you tried." And even as these words were coming out of her mouth, an extraordinary idea was forming in her head. "Do you want to try again?"

"Of course I do," said Kimo.

"I mean, right now," said Pippa.

"Right now we've got more important things to do," said Kimo. "We have to rescue Penny, remember?"

"Of course I remember," said Pippa. "I'm saying, what if by breaking the island record you could rescue Penny?"

"Then I would break the island record." Kimo didn't miss a beat.

And that was when Pippa nodded toward the roof of the building and asked, "How high do you think that roof is?"

Practicing the pole vault had got Kimo used to judging heights. He sized up the roof. "Sixteen feet, five inches," he said. "Give or take a couple of inches."

"So if you used that bamboo pole to vault up onto that roof . . ." Pippa didn't even have to finish her sentence. Kimo knew exactly what she meant. If he vaulted a foot higher than he had ever vaulted before, he would land on the roof of the warehouse. And maybe once he was up there he would find a way into the building and they would have a chance to get to Penny before the adoption papers were signed.

"I'll do it," the boy said.

And so for the second time that day, Kimo faced a pole vault higher than the island pole vaulting record. This time he was in an asphalt parking lot with a bamboo pole instead of a proper pole-vaulting pole and with no real pit to plant the pole in at the end of his run. The odds were against him. Doesn't matter, the boy thought as he walked away from the building, measuring his strides. I've got to do it this time, for Penny.

He found the spot seventeen strides from where he would jump and he took his position, facing the building. Pippa had told Kim and Toby what was happening and they had stopped cutting bamboo long enough to come over and watch. They stood behind Kimo, too nervous to shout or chant his name. Instead they softly spoke their encouragement. "You got this," said Kim.

"Do it for Penny," said Toby.

Then Pippa offered, "You know what Penny would say."

"My do it," they all said at once.

Kimo closed his eyes and imagined his jump. *Swish, swish, pop, zow-wee,* he thought. Then he corrected himself: *Swish, swish, pop, Penny!* If I get up there, I might find a door and maybe we can get inside and rescue her. He lifted the front of his pole into place.

He began to run. *Swish, swish, pop, Penny! Swish, swish, pop, Penny! Swish, swish, pop, Penny!* He could feel the power in his legs as he counted his strides: one, two, three, four, five . . . before he knew it, he was at seventeen, and he was planting the pole on the ground and shoving his right arm forward while he yanked his left arm back.

He felt himself launched up into the air, legs first, and then his whole body was traveling in an arc up and up . . .

With a soft thud, he landed on the roof.

He had done it. He had broken the island pole vaulting record. But he wasn't thinking about that now. He was focused on his little sister. How could he get her back?

He walked over to the edge of the roof and peered down at Kim, Pippa, and Toby, who were jumping up and down, hugging each other with glee. "Is there a door?" Pippa called up at him.

"Not sure," said Kimo.

"Go look behind the air-conditioning unit," said Pippa. "That's where it would be." Kimo padded across the roof to the unit, which was as tall as he was, and ducked behind it. Sure enough, just as Pippa had predicted, there was a trapdoor. He grabbed the handle and swung it open. It was dark, but he could just barely make out a set of stairs. If he went down them, he might find his way through the building to the front door, where he could let the others in.

He peered down into the stairwell. He had no idea where the stairs led, but he stepped down into the darkness anyway, and lowered the door back over his head.

Moments later, Kimo was sliding back the bolt on the front door and swinging it open so that light from outside spilled into the front hallway of the recording studio, where gold and silver records hung on all of the walls. "Shh." He put a finger to his lips as the others hurried past him into the dark building.

"Did you see Penny?" Kim whispered. Her heart was beating fast, filled with the furious worry that they were too late to get the baby back.

"I didn't see anyone," Kimo said. "It's the weekend. No one's around."

"Tina and Clarice have got be in here, though, right?" asked Pippa. "I mean, the cars are out front."

Suddenly they heard a deep low laugh. Toby immediately headed toward it. When he got to the end of the hallway, he found Leon seated in front of a small television in a lunch room. He was watching the Fitzgerald-Trouts' favorite soap opera, *Island Life*. On screen, Layla was standing between the twins—Kai and Jack—trying to decide which one she really loved, but before she could make her choice, Leon clicked off the set and looked up, saying in his very formal voice, "I was beginning to wonder if you might not return."

"The door was locked." Toby crossed his arms over his chest and glared at the driver.

"Oh, my goodness," said Leon. "They must have come up and locked it. I'm terribly sorry, and I'm glad you found another route in. You know, I considered leaving one of the limousines for you up in the vehicular parking area on the mountain."

"Leave me a limo?" asked Toby. "Why?"

"Ms. Clarice has three," said Leon, in his slow, comforting baritone. "She would hardly notice, and I thought if you didn't find your brothers and sisters, you might require it."

Toby was about to say that he didn't know how to drive, but Kim interrupted him. "We're looking for our sister."

"I believe she's downstairs. With a lawyer, who arrived some time ago," Leon said.

Hearing this, Kim's heart began to hammer in

her chest. She made herself ask, "Have they signed the papers yet?"

"I don't think they have, as they haven't got anything to sign with. Ms. Clarice came up here looking for a pen because the lawyer forgot to bring one."

"Did she find one?"

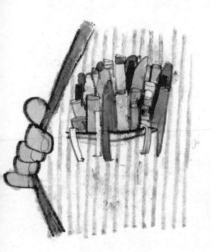

"She did not," said Leon. "Somehow all the pens in the building went missing." He opened his jacket and pulled out the handful of pens that he had hidden there. He grinned.

"I thought you might be coming, so I bought you as much extra time as I could."

"Thanks," said Toby, patting the limo driver on the back.

"Which way?" Kim asked, already charging out the door.

"Across the hall, you go through that door and you'll find a set of stairs down to a hall that leads to the recording studio." As the children raced from the room and started down the staircase, they heard him say, "Watch out for the bodyguards!"

Thank goodness he had warned them. If he hadn't, they would have dashed straight down the stairs and caught the guards' attention right away. Because of Leon's tip-off, the children stopped at the foot of the stairs and waited. They heard the voices of the guards coming through an open doorway down the hall. One of the bodyguards was saying, "Go directly to jail, do not pass go, do not collect two hundred dollars."

Wide-eyed with horror, Toby looked at the others and in a hush asked, "They're sending somebody to jail?"

"I think," said Kim in a whisper, "they're playing Monopoly."

She gestured for the others to follow her as

she tiptoed to the doorway and peeked into the room. She was right. The bodyguards were huddled around a table, focused on an epic Monopoly game. One of them seemed to be on a winning streak, and the other three were agonizing over each roll of the dice, wondering just how close it would bring them to bankruptcy.

The children exchanged knowing looks. They had been involved in many such Monopoly games, and they understood just how focused the players were on the outcome of each turn. The way to get past the open door without being spotted by the guards was obvious to all of them. They gestured to each other to confirm the plan, then they listened for the next roll of the dice. As soon as they heard it—just when they knew that all of the guards would have their eyes trained on the game board—the children dropped to the ground and crawled past the open door.

Once across, they jumped to their feet and ran to the end of the hallway, where they found a heavy metal door with a sign on it (in Serif font, Pippa couldn't help noticing) that said:

RECORDING STUDIO—
DO NOT ENTER IF LIGHT IS FLASHING

The red light over the door *was* flashing, but that didn't stop them. The Fitzgerald-Trout children flung it open and raced in.

They found themselves in a room with thickly padded walls, where Tina, her bouffant hairdo bobbing back and forth, was talking into a microphone that hung from the ceiling. The room was filled with instruments, including a large drum set, and on the far end of it, on the other side of all those instruments, Penny was sitting in a small open-topped cage.

As soon as the baby saw her siblings, she pulled herself up to her feet and began rocking the cage, which the children could now see was actually a playpen. Kim started toward the baby, but

Clarice—wearing her pointy high heels—came out of nowhere and stepped on Kim's bare foot.

"Ow!" Kim yelped, grabbing her foot and in the process knocking a guitar off its stand. It fell with a crash. When the guitar noise had faded away, they heard what Tina was saying into the microphone: ". . . I allow custody of Penny Fitzgerald-Trout to transfer to Baby Loves . . ."

But they didn't hear the rest because Kim lunged for the microphone and batted it away from Tina even as Pippa began to holler, "Give a loud shout . . ." Pippa had realized that if Tina wasn't able to be heard, then the recording she was

making wouldn't matter. "'Cause we're Fitzgerald-Trouts. We don't give up and we don't give in. We eat chocolate radishes and chicken skin!"

Kimo and Kim joined in on the next round of chanting, and so did Toby, who was so relieved to see Penny that he also jumped onto the drum set and grabbed the sticks. He began to bang on the drums with abandon as the siblings all screamed in unison, "We don't give up and we don't give in. We eat chocolate radishes and chicken skin!"

The baby rocked her playpen back and forth in time to the ruckus. "What the heck do you think you're doing?" Tina hollered.

"We're stopping you from what *you're* doing," Kim shouted back. "You're trying to give Penny away. You're recording some kind of legal thing."

The lawyer, Mr. Lawman, was sitting at one of the keyboards with his papers spread out in front of him. "A voice recording *is* a binding document," he said, adjusting the lapels of his suit jacket. He seemed utterly unfazed by the chaos.

"Doesn't matter!" Kim yelled at him. As if in agreement, Penny knocked her playpen onto its side so that she was free to crawl out of it. Kim, Kimo, and Pippa couldn't get to her because Clarice—and her dangerous footwear—were blocking the way, but they saw that if Penny could crawl through the tangle of instruments, then one of them would be able to reach down and scoop her up.

But of course Penny didn't know how to crawl. The baby just sat there on the floor. Toby had stopped drumming and was surreptitiously gesturing to her while mouthing the words, "Crawl, Penny. Come on. Crawl." The baby only blinked. She didn't move.

Kimo, meanwhile, had spotted the red RECORD button on the microphone and switched it into the OFF position. Kim had her hands on her hips and was shouting at Tina, Clarice, and the lawyer, "You can't give our baby away to Baby Loves because Baby Loves doesn't love our baby."

"Hey." Clarice smiled her tight smile. "That's a catchy jingle. Too bad I don't like what you're selling." This made Tina laugh. And that irritated Kim.

"We're not selling anything," Kim said in a voice like cement—hard, uniform, dependable, and completely unafraid. Now that the machine wasn't recording she didn't need to yell.

"Baby Loves is the finest baby product line on the whole island," Clarice said. "Good food. Good clothes. Good accessories. I've seen where you live and believe me, your sister will be better off with us. Baby Loves can offer her so much more than you can."

"No," said Kim, once again speaking clearly and solemnly. "It can't. Because we're not selling anything. That's the difference between us and you. You like Penny's smile and her laugh and that cute look she gets when she's about to drool, because you want to use them to make money. But we don't. We just love her smile and her laugh and, yes, we love the way she drools. Maybe we don't have fancy baby food from jars and maybe we don't have fancy toys or clothes, but we have more. We have the four of us, who love playing with her and singing to her and cooking for her and who don't even mind changing her dirty diapers. Babies deserve to be with the people who cherish them and love them and who want to be loved *by* them. You might be called Baby Loves, but you don't know anything about loving babies."

Mr. Lawman stood up from his keyboard and adjusted his cuffs. "Nice speech," he said. "You should be a lawyer when you grow up."

Kim suddenly realized that she *had* made a speech. Calmly and articulately, she had found the words that she wanted to say and she had said them.

"That's right," said Tina. "You should be a lawyer."

I'm good at public speaking, Kim thought. I'm never going to worry about it again. Tina was smiling at her, and Kim thought for a second that perhaps Tina had been convinced by her words. Perhaps Tina did want what was best for Penny and perhaps Tina now understood that what was best for Penny was being with her siblings. Kim watched as Tina pulled a compact mirror out of her pocket and checked her reflection, then slid a tube of lipstick out of her purse and expertly painted her lips. When she'd finished, she pressed them together into a kiss, saying, "You should definitely be a lawyer when you grow up. But you're not grown up yet, are you, Kimberly?"

"My name is not Kimberly," said Kim. "It's Kim."

"Whatever it is," said Tina, "you're just a child. A minor. And minors can't be lawyers and they can't take care of babies." She turned to Mr. Lawman. "Isn't that right?"

"That's right," said the lawyer. "Minors have no legal claim to custody of other minors."

Kim realized with horror that her speech

hadn't mattered. Tina was too terrible to care what was best for Penny. There's no speech that will ever convince her to do the right thing, Kim thought. But she was not going to let Tina have the last word. She shook her fist and said, "If being a grown-up means being like the three of you, none of us ever wants to be one."

Inspired by her older sister, Pippa charged past Clarice (and her high heels) straight into the tangle of instruments. She waded toward Penny, who was sitting on the floor near the overturned playpen. Words hadn't worked, so Pippa had decided she would extract the baby from the room by force.

But it wasn't meant to be. Tina swung open the door to the recording studio and shouted down the hallway, "We have a situation!" Seconds later, the four bodyguards appeared in the doorway. They each took hold of one of the four Fitzgerald-Trouts and they carried them—struggling and shouting—from the room.

The late afternoon sun slanted low through the windshield of the car where the Fitzgerald-Trout children sat gathering themselves and watching the front doors of the recording studio. They were trying to stay out of sight while they decided what to do next. They knew that there was no way to go back into the building, since the bodyguards had taken up positions in the front hallway. And they suspected that even if Kimo could pole vault onto the roof again and sneak back down the stairs, he wouldn't be able to get past the bodyguards and down to the basement to extract the baby. No matter how many times they mulled over the situation, they couldn't see a way to get to Penny.

Kim was drumming her hands on the steering wheel. "We could wait until they come out of the building?"

"We've been through this," said Kimo, who was watching the doors through the binoculars. "They'll have the bodyguards with them."

"We have to get her when no one's paying attention." This was Pippa, whose stomach was growling with hunger. It had been hours since any of them had eaten, but they weren't letting themselves think about anything but their little sister. "Maybe we can get to her when she's back at that hotel."

"No," said Kim. "That'll be too late. Clarice won't take her back there till the lawyer has finished the recording, so Baby Loves will have custody of her by then."

"So what?" said Toby, who had pulled a large

piece of foam out of the hole in the seat and was shredding it to pieces. "Who cares about that?"

"We care," said Kim. "She's ours, not theirs."

"But recordings and paperwork, that's just grown-up stuff." Toby lifted his feet and pressed them against the back of Kim's seat. "All that matters is Penny."

Maybe they were light-headed with hunger or maybe they were exhausted from a long day or maybe Toby was entirely right, because all of a sudden they all felt that what Toby had said was true. Only grown-ups worried about legal documents and paperwork, and they weren't grown-ups—as Tina herself had just pointed out to them. All they needed to worry about was getting Penny back into their arms.

"So we wait it out and let Clarice take her back to the Baby Loves office," Kimo said. "Then when Clarice has stopped paying attention, when she thinks we've given up, we sneak into the office and take her back."

Energized by this plan, Kim sat up straighter in her seat. "Toby, what's the office like? And Pippa, listen up, because you're the one who got us into the recording studio."

Pippa nodded as Toby said, "There's an elevator that goes right up to it from the lobby of the hotel." He was remembering their ride when Penny had compared the elevator to a limo.

"Perfect," said Pippa.

"You need a little plastic thingy to unlock it so that you can press the button for the right floor."

"Not perfect," said Pippa. "That's going to be tricky to get around."

"Maybe we should go back to the Castle," said Kim. "Toby can draw a map of the hotel and we'll figure out what to do next."

"So we're leaving Penny here?" Pippa's voice was thin with apprehension. Even though she agreed with the plan, she could not actually imagine driving away and leaving the littlest Fitzgerald-Trout with Clarice and Tina.

"We have to." Kimo was emphatic. "They have to think we've given up if we're going to be able to sneak into the hotel."

They all agreed but nevertheless a blue mood settled over them as Kim turned the key to start the car. The mood was made worse by the sound they heard next . . . not *grrrg*, not *sputter*, not even *clunk*, but a hollow *click, click, click*. The key was turning in the ignition, but the car's engine didn't make a sound.

After several attempts, Kim took her hand from the ignition and shook her head, saying,

"That's it, the engine's . . ." She choked on the end of her sentence. She could not say the word that she was thinking.

The little green car had been almost like another member of their family. It had given them shelter, warmth, comfort. It had transported them, and now it was . . . well, it was . . . she shuddered with horror as Kimo made the pronouncement: "Dead."

There was a long moment of sorrowful silence, broken when a fly flew through Toby's open window and up between the front seats and began to hurl itself against the windshield. The violent buzzing brought them back to their senses.

"How about a tow truck?" Kim asked.

"We can't afford it," said Kimo.

"So we're, what? Leaving the car here?" asked Pippa. "Walking back to the Castle?"

"I guess so," said Kim.

But Toby was already opening his door and getting out of the car. "No," he said. "That's not what we're doing." He walked purposefully across the parking lot between the rows of parked cars.

"Where are you going?" Kim called out even as she saw exactly where Toby was headed. He was swinging open the door of Clarice's limo. The boy disappeared inside. For a second all they could see were the soles of his feet, then he popped back out of the limo holding up the keys triumphantly. The others climbed out of the little green car and ran across the parking lot to join him.

"But we can't just take it," Kimo said.

"We're borrowing it," said Toby. "Leon told us we could. You heard him, he said Clarice has three limos."

Kim didn't need to be convinced. She grabbed the keys from Toby and clambered into the front seat, where she found Leon's hat. She slipped it onto her head. "Let's go!"

"What about our stuff?" Pippa asked.

"Right," said Kim, and they went back to the little green car to gather their belongings.

A few minutes later they were speeding along the coastal road, heading for the Muldoon Park Parking Lot. The limo went much faster than the little green car had ever gone, and though she had to really concentrate to steer it around corners, Kim found it otherwise very easy to drive. The engine was loud and responsive; she barely had to touch the gas to feel the car surging ahead.

Kimo sat beside her, eating a bag of peanuts, drinking a guava juice, and anxiously pressing the button that raised and lowered the glass window between the front seat and the back. It was only after he'd climbed into his customary seat in the front that he realized that Pippa and Toby—in back—now had much better seats than he did. If the car weren't already moving, he would have taken off his seat belt and climbed into the back, where his siblings had their legs stretched out and their heads reclined. They were staring up through the open sunroof at the pink clouds sliding by. On another night, they might have all been jubilantly celebrating the fun of having a new vehicle filled with food and juice, but with Penny gone the mood was somber. No one felt like listening to the radio or watching the little TV set. Toby thought about the show he had watched the first time he'd seen the limousine. About the rabbit that had lost his ears. Losing Penny felt like that, like losing a part of himself.

When they arrived at the parking lot, Kim expertly maneuvered the limo into a space. Then she rolled up the windows, closed the sunroof, and turned the engine off. She took off Leon's hat and left it on the seat.

As the sun slid behind the mountain, they took their first steps onto the trail that led to the Castle. Kim thought about how only weeks before, they'd been nervous to hike up the mountain in darkness. Now they were sure-footed and unafraid. They knew exactly where they were going. And they knew for certain that at the end of the trail, their home awaited them. But even this thought did not make her feel content. There was a Penny-sized

hole in their family, and until they got the baby back, everything they did together would be robbed of happiness.

Kimo switched on the flashlight and trained the beam at their feet so everyone could see the contours of the trail. There was no singing as they walked, just the steady *clomp* of bare feet on ground. When they got to the mound of hardened lava, they marched up and over it, and Kim thought again of their first trek up the mountain and the night they'd spent at the mouth of the cave, cooking hot dogs. She remembered burning the page with the words about Captain Baker's ghost. As this memory rose in her mind, so did a terrifying thought: The scythe-footed ghost-monster was still out there. She turned and touched Pippa on the shoulder, quietly saying, "Ah, Pips? Maybe we shouldn't go back to the Castle."

"Why not?" Toby had overheard.

Pippa knew exactly what Kim meant. "Let it eat us," the little girl said morosely.

"Don't say that." Kimo stabbed the darkness with the flashlight. "If we're going to rescue Penny tomorrow, we can't be eaten by a monster tonight."

Toby didn't like the sound of this. "What are you talking about?" he asked, but no one answered. They arrived at the edge of the forest and in the deep blue of twilight, they could see the great dark hulk of the Castle across the open field.

"We may as well keep going." This was Pippa. "We've slept there a lot and it hasn't eaten us yet."

"*What* hasn't eaten us? What? What?" Toby couldn't stand it anymore. "Tell me what you're talking about." So Kim, Pippa, and Kimo quickly explained to Toby about the scythe-shaped prints and their theory that they belonged to a rustling ghost-monster.

"Great," said Toby. "Terrific."

"So what should we—" Kim was about to say "do" but was stopped by a sound from across the field. A long, high-pitched, hair-raising wail, the wail of something not at all human. "It's coming from inside the Castle," Kim said as terror flooded her body.

K imo switched off the flashlight and pulled the others so close that their knees were touching. "Let's get out of here," he said.

"I don't like this," whispered Toby even as they heard the sound of the cry again.

But Pippa broke free of the tangle of arms. Something about the sound made her picture the whale on the piece of scrimshaw. "It's in pain," she said. "We have to help."

"Help a monster?" Kimo yelped.

"It's our duty," said Pippa.

Just then, Toby gave a shout. "Goldie!" The boy had remembered his goldfish, left in its jar in the Castle. He dashed out into the field. He wasn't going to let the ghost-monster mess with his pet. Pippa grabbed the flashlight from Kimo and took off after him.

A moment later, Toby flew through the door of the Castle and saw that something enormous was on the floor, writhing in the darkness. He couldn't

tell what it was, but he rushed blindly around the edges of the room, heading for the hint of moonlight that glinted off Goldie's jar. When he got there, he lifted the jar off the fireplace and gave a great sigh of relief as he held the fish close to his heart.

But what was on the floor? Standing on the other side

of the room, Pippa trained the flashlight on the struggling mass, and now they saw that whatever it was, it was trapped in a web of ropes and sails.

"The hammocks, the canopies," said Pippa. "It's tangled."

But what was it? What was the rustling, scythe-footed ghost-monster that made such a terrible keening sound? It was too covered in sails and hammocks for Pippa to see exactly what it was. Still, Pippa thought it sounded more hurt than it did dangerous. She screwed up her courage and padded across the moss till she was kneeling beside it. With a sudden yank, she pulled a sail away from where she thought its face might be.

What she saw made her laugh.

She looked up at the others, her eyes opened wide in disbelief. "It's not a mon-ster at all," she said. "It's a giraffe."

And so it was. A giraffe that had escaped from the Wildlife Safari Park when all the fences were knocked down by the flooding. A giraffe who, Kim now pointed out, had hooves shaped like two scythes.

Pippa held the giraffe's head in her lap as she explained. "Bronco Bragg said he and some other cowboys rode all over the mountain trying to track the animals down and round them up." She was stroking the giraffe and whispering to it sweetly as the others slowly and carefully untangled the ropes and sails from around its body. The animal's frightening wail had turned into a whimper. Pippa read the tag on the giraffe's collar. "Zephyr," she said. "What a good name." Almost as if in answer to that, the giraffe stopped whimpering and licked Pippa's cheek with his long purple tongue, a tongue as rough as sandpaper. It made the girl giggle.

"He's only a year old," said Kim. "The tag's got his birthday stamped right on it."

"He must have been scared, all by himself, without his family," Kimo mused.

Toby clutched his goldfish even more tightly to his chest.

As the last sail was being untangled from the giraffe, Kimo discovered Pippa's knickknack shelf in the mess. The giraffe had knocked it down when he was stumbling around the Castle caught in the web, but the shelf was so well-constructed that it was still in one piece. Kimo handed it to Pippa, who brushed the dirt off it and placed it on the mantel above the cooking fireplace. Then she put the two pieces of scrimshaw on it. "I'd feel better if we all shared them," she said.

"They're awesome," said Kim. "But they're yours. You should put them wherever you want." There was something about the baby being missing that made them all want to be extra kind to each other.

Perhaps the baby giraffe sensed this too, because when he had shrugged off the last of the sails and risen up on his four unexpectedly long legs, he did not bolt out the door but bent his long neck down and licked each one of the children on the forehead with that purple tongue. Then he slowly crossed the mossy floor and reached up his head toward one of the trees that grew into the Castle. He began to eat the leaves.

Now the children heard the rustle and the slurp that they had heard that terrifying night a few weeks before. The slurping was the sound his hooves made in the mud and moss. The rustle was the sound his mouth made chewing the leaves.

"Some monster," said Kimo.

"I bet we scared him as much as he scared us." Pippa laughed.

"I hope he'll stay," said Kim. The Penny-sized hole in their family wouldn't be any smaller with the creature there, but Kim was comforted by the thought of taking care of another baby—even if it was a giraffe.

They spent the rest of the night eating macaroni and cheese (made in a pot over the campfire) and coming up with a plan to rescue Penny the following day. They all agreed that they should descend on the Royal Palm hotel first thing in the morning—before they'd even eaten breakfast—when the employees were still sleepy and wouldn't pay as much attention to them. Kim had Leon's hat (it was on the seat of the limousine), so she would be in costume as a limo driver and would be able to go downstairs to the room in the hotel where the employees and drivers watched television. Toby remembered hearing about this room and was certain that as long as Kim had the hat on, everyone would think that she belonged there. Meanwhile Toby, Kimo, and Pippa would go to the hotel lobby. Toby thought he remembered a phone on the wall, and he was pretty sure it could be used to order room service.

That so much of this plan hinged on Toby's memory of his one afternoon in the hotel made the older Fitzgerald-Trouts nervous. Since most of the boy's clearest memories seemed to focus on the room service menu, Pippa made a case for using room service as a way to get into Clarice's office. Her idea was that once Kim was downstairs in the employee television room, she should find her way to the kitchen. Pippa, Toby, and Kimo would use the phone in the lobby to order room service for Clarice. Just before the order was supposed to be ready, Kim would pretend she was one of the bellhops and volunteer to deliver the order to Clarice's penthouse. Toby told Kim that if she could find a bright green bellhop's jacket and put it on, the plan would go off without a hitch.

Pippa guessed that once Kim was given the room service cart, she would also be given the little plastic key thingy to unlock the elevator button to Clarice's floor. On her way up from the kitchen, in the elevator, Kim could stop at the lobby and let the others—Toby, Kimo, and Pippa—onto the elevator.

They would ride together to Clarice's penthouse and when the elevator door opened, they would be in the foyer of Baby Loves. If Penny was there, they would take her. If not, they would try the office of Baby Loves, which Toby thought he remembered was through the doors on the left.

They stayed up late that night reviewing the plan, talking through every possible complication. As they talked, they curled up beside the baby giraffe, who, after his satisfying meal of leaves, had fallen asleep on the moss.

"It's not a flawless plan," said Pippa.

"Few plans are." Kimo was trying to be hopeful.

"How close is the TV break room to the kitchen?" Kim asked Toby.

"It's right next door," said Toby.

"How do you know?" asked Pippa. "You were only ever upstairs."

"Goldie was down there with Leon and he told me," Toby answered matter-of-factly.

"Goldie told you?" The older three rolled over and looked at Toby.

"Wait a second," said Pippa. "Are you telling us that this plan we've come up with is based upon telepathic communication with a fish?"

"Yeah," said Toby. "So?"

Kim poked Pippa in the shoulder as if to say *be nice.* "Well," said Pippa, "if anybody can read a fish's mind, it's you." What else was there to say? If there was one thing they were learning from the Family Monster Calamity, it was to rely on each other's strengths and to always give each other the benefit of the doubt.

Through all of this planning, Zephyr was a comforting presence. His warm back rose and fell with his breath; Kimo was reminded of their nights sleeping on the boat. Maybe we'll never get that boat, he thought. Doesn't matter. As long as we're all together again.

As if Kim had read his mind, she said, "Don't worry. We're going to get Penny back."

CHAPTER

20

High up in the penthouse of the Royal Palm hotel, the baby lay on her back in a Baby Loves designer crib listening to a Baby Loves mobile play "Twinkle, Twinkle, Little Star" as four little plastic stars rotated in the air above her.

Those aren't real stars, Penny thought to herself (even as she realized for the first time that she knew the word for stars). Those aren't like stars at all. The baby thought about how the sky looked when she lay in her hammock in the Castle and stared at it through the gaps in the sailcloth roof. She thought about the sounds of her brothers and sisters sleeping nearby. Those sounds were much more comforting than the mobile churning out its mechanical tune. And where were they now, her brothers and sisters? What had happened?

She knew that they had tried to come and get her when she'd been in that loud room with all the instruments. She'd been so happy when they had suddenly rushed through the door and charged toward her. They'd made a lot of noise—shouting and banging on drums—and the grown-ups had been confused and upset. For a little while, it had seemed that Penny would go home with her brothers and sisters. But then, just as suddenly as they had arrived, the older children had been taken away.

When were they coming back? And what if they didn't come back? What if they couldn't get to her?

It was clear to the baby just exactly what she had to do.

Grabbing hold of the crib's railing, she pulled herself to her feet and began to rock from side to side, just as she had done in the recording studio. The mobile and its stars swung back and forth; the base of the crib lifted off the floor, and just as it lifted, Penny threw herself against the opposite side, tipping the crib over.

Hurrah! She had done it. The crib was toppled and she had fallen out and was sitting on the floor, staring at her own two feet. But what needed to happen next was the hard part. She had to get across the room to the kitchen. Which meant that she had to move across the floor on her own. But the baby wasn't sure she knew how to do that.

She sat on the floor holding onto her toes and thinking about this for so long that by the time she had an answer, there was a pool of drool in front of her. She had to do what Toby had done when he'd been on the ground, in the moss, saying, "Crawl, crawl, crawl." She remembered that he had wiggled himself: one arm and the opposite leg working and then the other arm and the other leg working.

"Quall," she said out loud, and then she tried it. Wiggling one arm and the opposite leg. The other arm, the other leg. It worked. "Quall!" she shouted, and then she heard the song in her head—"Give a loud shout, 'cause we're Fitzgerald-Trouts . . ."— and she sang it to herself as she began to make her way forward.

She was very pleased with her progress as she found herself moving across the floor to the kitchen cupboards, where she knew that she would find the pots and pans that Clarice used to heat up

baby food. She would get her hands on those pots and pans. She would use them to make noise just like the older kids had done when they had upset and confused the adults. If she could do this, if she could make a terrible racket, she was sure that she could rescue herself.

We don't give up and we don't give in, she sang to herself as she reached the kitchen cupboards.

CHAPTER
21

Despite the warmth of the giraffe beside them and the soft moss beneath them, the eldest four Fitzgerald-Trouts slept very badly, tossing and turning so much that small twigs tangled in their hair and leaves pressed into their skin. Each of them had some version of a nightmare in which he or she was trying to rescue Penny but could not get to her in time. One by one, they woke from these awful dreams and lay in the clammy darkness, talking quietly to each other as they waited for the first hint of sunlight that meant they could hike down the mountain and put their rescue plan into action.

But they never got this chance, because as those first streaks of light broke through the branches overhead, they heard a startling scream. They were on their feet instantly. Pippa thought something had happened to Zephyr, but then she realized that he was beside her on *his* feet, also surprised by the noise. She rubbed her eyes and followed the others, who were stumbling out of the Castle.

As they emerged into the field, the children saw something so amazing that they clung to each other, wondering if it was a dream. Wearing her ridiculous high heels and her snakeskin jumpsuit, Clarice was charging out of the woods toward them. In her arms she held Penny, who was screeching at the top of her lungs and pulling on the woman's hair.

Halfway across the clearing, Clarice stopped to catch her breath and to untangle the baby's fists from her curly locks. She looked up and saw the four older Fitzgerald-Trouts standing there, staring at her. "How am I supposed to deal with this?" she shouted as she lowered the baby into the field of purple orchids.

The older children were still blinking awake and trying to understand what was happening, but they all saw that the baby had an enormous smile on her face. What had she done?

"I wanted a baby," Clarice said. "A cute baby. I didn't want a child who wakes me up banging pots and pans and when I try to calm her down with a bottle of milk spits it up all over me. Snakeskin is very hard to clean." She gestured to a large milky stain on her pantsuit. "Then when I put her down, she goes everywhere . . ."

And that's when Kim, Kimo, Pippa, and Toby saw that it was true; still smiling her enormous smile, Penny was also moving toward them on all fours. The baby was crawling, and Clarice was fuming. "She doesn't stay still for a second. How am I supposed to use her for a photo shoot if she won't stay still?" Clarice lifted her foot and scraped the mud off her high heels on a nearby stump. "You have to take her back." The four older Fitzgerald-Trouts took in this new development with amazement; there would be no rescue at the Royal Palm hotel because Penny had rescued herself.

"I've got a business to run," Clarice said, turning and starting back down the hill.

"I hope you learned your lesson," Kim called out. "A business has no business adopting a baby." They all looked across the field at Penny, who was still moving on all fours toward them. Toby felt his heart surge with joy. He knelt down in the moss, watching as Penny got closer. He knew he had to resist the urge to run to her and scoop her up. Penny had earned the right to arrive under her own steam.

When she got to Toby, the baby looked at him and said, "Hi." Toby laughed and pulled her into his arms, then he got to his feet and the four siblings formed a small huddle around their littlest member.

"My do it," Penny chirped, feeling smug about just how perfectly her plan had worked.

"Yes, you did," Kim said.

"Let's promise to never lose each other again," said Kimo. The others nodded, and Pippa sang out, "Give a loud shout—" Suddenly into the huddle poked a small yellow-and-brown head. It was Zephyr, blinking his enormous eyes with their long lashes. The siblings looked at each other and sang out together, "We've got a giraffe!" Then they all shouted different things: "He fits right in," "He always grins," "He's lost his kin." And Toby tried, "We named him Tim," which made them all laugh, especially Penny, who understood every word the older children were saying.

EPILOGUE

It was several months later, at a small party celebrating the birth of Mr. Knuckles's and Asha's baby, that I first heard this story from the Fitzgerald-Trouts. We were eating doughnuts and drinking papaya juice and the whole room was filled with the warm, pleasant scent of dryers (a number of the guests had brought laundry to do during the party). I was telling Kimo that I had been away from the island and was sorry I'd missed his attempt to break the island record.

"Doesn't matter," the boy said.

"I hope you'll try again," I offered.

"He doesn't need to try again," Pippa said cryptically, and her siblings all laughed. I must have looked confused because the next thing I knew they were telling me the story of Kimo's jump onto the roof of the record studio.

"That's wonderful," I said. "I hope you told Ms. Bonicle."

"Yeah," said Kimo. "She was happy. She's gonna set up another track meet so I can do it in front of a crowd."

Then it occurred to me to ask, "Why in the heck were you trying to break into the record studio anyway?" They looked at each other—one to another—as if they were making sure everyone agreed, and then they quickly filled me in on their adventure finding the Castle and how things between them had gone wrong after they'd found it.

"We love the Castle," said Kim. "But family is the most important home."

"It's true," said Kimo.

"But that doesn't mean we aren't fixing the Castle up," Pippa added. She explained that her shop teacher, Bronco Bragg, had helped her sell a piece of scrimshaw that she'd found to buy a big load of lumber and nails and tools. He and a limo driver named Leon were helping the children build walls and a proper roof for the Castle.

"We were trying to decide if we should just have one big room or if we should have separate rooms," Kimo said. "Then we realized the Castle is so big that we can have both."

"My room will have a shelf where I can put Goldie's jar," said Toby, gesturing to the goldfish who he'd brought with him to the laundromat.

"And we can have a kitchen," said Kim. "With shelves and a table and chairs." She was holding onto Penny's hands and the little baby was standing on her own two feet. She was going to be walking any day now. "It's going to be a proper home, and we're going to use proper table manners." Kim gave a grin.

Pippa rolled her eyes. "Ever since Kim got an A

on her speech, eating with her is no fun." I could see that Pippa was only trying to sound annoyed when really she was proud of her older sister.

Just then Asha brushed past us, carrying her tiny daughter in her arms. She smiled radiantly. "It's time to announce the baby's name." She and Mr. Knuckles had not told anyone what they were calling their little girl.

"You're not naming her Baby Girl, are you?" asked Kim.

"I wouldn't be smiling like this if we were," said Asha.

"Fitzgerald-Trouts, where are you?" Mr. Knuckles called out from his spot over by the cash register. He was holding up his glass of papaya juice like he was preparing to make a toast.

"Over here," the children said, waving to him.

"These kids best parents we know," he said to the assembled guests. "And they name their baby Penny."

"Find a penny, pick it up, all day long you'll have good luck," Asha sang out across the crowd.

"We want good luck too," said Mr. Knuckles. "So we name our daughter . . . Nickel." He lifted his glass even higher. "To Nickel Knuckles."

"Nickel Knuckles," they all chorused. The baby in Asha's arms was curled up with her eyes closed shut. She was too sleepy to care what her name was yet.

"Awesome name," said Toby, and the rest of us agreed.

Now Asha spoke to the assembled guests. "The Fitzgerald-Trout children have offered to teach us a few things about how to be good parents. So we wanted to ask . . ." She turned to look at the children. "Would you be Nickel's godparents?"

I was watching the Fitzgerald-Trouts and I saw the effect these words had on them. They wiped the doughnut crumbs from their lips and straightened their backs, then Kim stepped forward and said, "Of course we would. We'd be thrilled." She began to describe to all of us what terrific parents she thought Mr. Knuckles and Asha would make. She talked about their kindness, their generosity, their love—all qualities essential to being a good parent. At the end of her speech, Kim raised her glass and said, "To Asha and Mr. Knuckles and their baby girl." Everyone repeated Kim's words, clinked their glasses, and drank their juice.

The party began to break up. The children filled their backpacks with their clean laundry and said their goodbyes, then they headed for the door. I trailed behind them.

"I'm thinking of writing another book," I said. "What would you say to letting me tell this story?" They looked at each other and again seemed to communicate without speaking. "We could meet somewhere you like," I said. "I'll bring ginker cake." I knew it was their favorite.

"It wouldn't be a bad thing for other kids to know what happened to us," said Kim. "How we almost lost each other." No one disagreed.

"How's next Sunday?" I asked.

"There's a fishing stream that we like," said Kimo. He told me exactly where it was and we agreed on a time for our picnic. Then they started across the parking lot, where mynah birds were bathing in the rain puddles.

"Is there any chance I could meet Zephyr?" I said.

"Oh no," said Pippa, looking back at me. "After what happened to us, we knew we couldn't keep him. We took him back to his family."

"You took him back?"

"Bronco Bragg knew where they were. In that new animal safari park on the North Shore. We drove him there ourselves," she added. "In the limo. His neck fit right through the sunroof."

With that, they turned their backs on me and walked toward the long black car. Toby holding his goldfish. Kimo holding the baby. Pippa and Kim carrying backpacks full of clean laundry.

"See you soon," I called out. When they didn't

say anything, I tried again. "I see you've still got the limo."

It was Kimo who turned back this time, squinting at me and saying, "Clarice hasn't even noticed. Can you imagine that?" He smiled and I swear the baby in his arms winked at me. Then they all climbed into the limousine and I watched them drive away.

THANK-YOUS

My deepest thanks to the Fitzgerald-Trout children, who let me tell this story. To my invaluable readers: Solomon Alba, Gemma Fudge, Jozy Liftin-Harris, Silas Liftin-Harris, Sara O'Leary, Hilary Liftin, Finn Sanders, Graley Sanders, Kristin Sanders, Linda Spalding, Augie Thorne, Sylvie Thorne, and Serena Zarin. Thanks to Liam Temple for Ms. Bonicle. To Anastasios Theodorou for his insights into pole vaulting. To the incomparable Gregg Gellman, Jerry Kalajian, and Jackie Kaiser. To Jen Dana, for her belief. To Lee Gatlin, for bringing the book to life. To Susan Rich, with me from the beginning. To Tara Walker, Peter Phillips, John Martz, and especially Lynne Missen, without whom this book would not exist. To Semi Chellas, the greatest collaborator a writer could ask for. To Douglas, always. And finally, thanks to Philip E. Spalding III (Pea Tree) for the memories.